IT'S BETTER TO LAUGH THAN TO CRY

John Seland

authorHOUSE

AuthorHouse™
1663 Liberty Drive
Bloomington, IN 47403
www.authorhouse.com
Phone: 1 (800) 839-8640

© *2019 John Seland. All rights reserved.*

No part of this book may be reproduced, stored in a retrieval system, or transmitted by any means without the written permission of the author.

Published by AuthorHouse 04/18/2019

ISBN: 978-1-5462-7292-2 (sc)
ISBN: 978-1-5462-7293-9 (e)

Library of Congress Control Number: 2018914883

Print information available on the last page.

Any people depicted in stock imagery provided by Getty Images are models, and such images are being used for illustrative purposes only. Certain stock imagery © Getty Images.

This book is printed on acid-free paper.

Because of the dynamic nature of the Internet, any web addresses or links contained in this book may have changed since publication and may no longer be valid. The views expressed in this work are solely those of the author and do not necessarily reflect the views of the publisher, and the publisher hereby disclaims any responsibility for them.

CONTENTS

SOMETHING IN COMMON

"Hi, Mom!"

"Hi! You're home early tonight."

"Un-huh. Got a ride from Billy. He was passing Dunmore."

"That's good! How was work today?"

"About the same. Except, the boss put me at the register. Can't figure it out. He knows I'm afraid of people." (Laughing)

"Oh, come on! You've not afraid of me."

"That's right, Mom, except when you drive. You always drive with your eyes closed." (More laughter)

"Oh, I almost forgot. The Walsh's have a guest—a priest, no, a brother. I told him about you. He said he'd like to meet you. Can you go and say hello?"

"OK, tomorrow."

"He mentioned tonight. Go ahead. I'll warm the spaghetti and meatballs."

About twenty minutes later, he returns.

"Ah, smells good!"

"How was it?"

"Not bad. He's a nice guy. I'll see him tomorrow."

He eats slowly, glancing at the newspaper to see if the Pirates won. About an hour later, he's falling asleep, eating spaghetti and wondering why the boss put him at the cash register.

Three weeks later, he was on top of a ladder, splashing paint on the eaves of Ford's two-story house. Try as he did, he couldn't stretch out as he'd like, thus another spot went by without some paint. Oh, well, he thought, nobody's perfect, especially twenty-five feet above the ground. Just then, he heard his mother calling. "Michael! You have a phone call—from New Jersey!"

New Jersey! Jeeze! As he hurried down the ladder, he remembered what the brother had said. "May I write a letter for you? I know the rector there. I can tell him you're interested in the priesthood."

Inside the kitchen, he took the phone.

"Hello, this is Michael White. Can I help you?"

The voice was deep and slow. "Oh, Michael, hello! This is Father Bischeimer, from Bordentown. I hope you're doing well. Listen, I just received a letter from Brother Richard Walsh. Said he met you recently."

"Yes, I know Brother Richard. We met last week."

"I see. Well, he wrote a rather complementary letter. He did mention a few, ah, *quirks*, though."

"Quirks?"

"Yes. Couldn't quite understand what he was getting at—something about you having certain *obsessions*."

"Obsessions?"

"Yes, you know, always talking about the same things. Mentioned something about you talking a lot about a cash register . . . oh, and something about *spaghetti and meatballs*. Sorry, but I haven't the slightest idea what he was getting at. Anyway, we decided to accept you. You see, well, to tell the truth, we're just a small place and we need accreditation. And to get that we numbers . . . *numbers*! So, well, as I said, we decided to accept you. Congratulations! Oh, one more thing. I know it's rather sudden but, can you come here on Sunday, I mean, this coming Sunday? We're starting a new school year on Monday. I'm sorry for the short notice."

Answering in a rather excited voice (since he doesn't have the slightest idea what a seminary is like), he blurted out: "Yes, yes, of course, of course! Sunday! Right! I'm there, I mean, I'll be there. Sunday, Right! Bye!"

His mother is ecstatic. "Oh, to have a priest in our family! Oh, oh, how wonderful! I never thought I'd see the day!"

"Well, Mom, let's not rush things. I'm not ordained yet. I mean, it'll take some time, I'm sure" (although he's not so sure). Then he starts counting on his fingers. "Let's see, Thursday. That's today. Tomorrow is Friday, then Saturday . . . Sunday." Then, suddenly, he's hit by an epiphany. "Oh, God! The house! I haven't finished the house! Jesus!"

A few seconds later, he's on the phone. "Billy, quick! Get over here! We've got to finish the house! I mean, I'm painting a house and, and . . . never mind, never mind. I'll explain later. Wear your old clothes!"

Two days later, on Saturday, with more paint on their trousers, shirts, and hands than on the house, they've finished. Then, having packed a few things, the only remaining item was the haircut. And so, towards evening, he made his way to the barbershop. When it was his turn, he took a seat. Then, holding his thumb and index finger close, he told the barber how he'd like his hair cut—"a bit short, please." That settled, he sat back and let the barber do his thing.

The barber was new and, as soon became apparent, very inquisitive. The questions came quickly, one after another.

"You live around here?"

"Yes, over there on Holly Road."

"Is that so? You're a student?"

"Well, not really. I was going to Johnson Trade School—taking up mechanics. But it wasn't so interesting—all the oil and stuff—so I quit."

"Is that so? Working somewhere?"

"Yes, at the A&P—part-time." Then he decided to share the news.

"Actually, I'm entering a seminary."

"A seminary? What kind of seminary?"

"The one in Bordentown—Divine Word."

"Divine Word? Never heard of it. Hey, are you sure? I mean, you never know. Those Mafia guys are everywhere. (Pause, as he clips away.) "You mean, you wanna be a priest?"

"I think so."

"Hey, that's great! But, wait! Those guys don't marry, do they? How're ya gonna handle that?"

"I don't know. Guess I'll have to wait and see."

"Hey, you know, I have a nephew. He's a semitarian, too. Started two years ago. Speaks Greece or somethin'. Gotta hand it to 'em. In grade school, he couldn't even memorize the 'Hail Mary.' But he told me . . . "

And all the while, the scissors kept busy—snip . . . snip . . . snip—sending him into a mild sleep. Thirty minutes or so later, he could feel the barber brushing off some hair. When he woke, he looked in the mirror. "Oh!" was the only word he could manage.

"Er, sorry!" said the barber. "Got caught up a little. But you said 'short,' right? Ha, ha!"

Oh, God! he thought. "They'll never let me in. Too old." Immediately, his mind switched to the statue in church—Saint Paul, bald as a bat. They had something in common.

On Sunday morning, as the car began to pull away, he gave a backward glance at the house. Patches of fading brown peeped through the new white paint. Thank goodness, Mr. Ford was nearsighted. Still, just to be sure, he told his parents not to give him his new address. He couldn't afford a lawyer.

Night Shift at the A&P

"Excuse me, Michael! Could you step in the office for a minute, that is, ah, after you finish wiping the floor?"

"Yes, sir, of course, right away!"

A minute later, he makes his way to the office, thinking he's in for a scolding for having spilled some water on the floor.

"Listen, Michael, I've been watching your performance. And to tell the truth, I'm impressed . . . very impressed. I mean, the way you do things so, so, ah, *efficiently.* That's it: so *efficiently.* That's what I like; that's just what I like. And so, well, to put it short, Michael, I'm giving you a promotion."

"Huh! You mean, you mean, sir, I'm really getting a promotion? You mean, I'm, ah, moving up the ladder?"

"That's right, Michael! It's step by step, of course, but there's no doubt about it, you're moving right up the ladder. And it all comes from your . . . your *efficiency.*"

"Gosh, sir, I, I don't know what to say. I mean, it's so sudden and so . . . so *unreal.*"

Yes, yes, I'm sure it is. But, ah, let me clarify. You see, I need someone for the night shift. Someone reliable, someone who can, ah, who can fill in. That's it: fill in. And, well, I know the right man when I see him. And, Michael, I'm happy to say it, *you are that man.* And I know that you will do a good job while always upholding our motto."

At this, both the manager and Michael put their right hand over their heart and begin to recite in a solemn tone the company's motto.

"Oh, A&P, oh, A&P!

We're all so happy at the A&P!

Never a worry, never a fear,

Because the A&P is always at our rear."

It was a trying moment, which could be seen when the manager quickly fetched his handkerchief and began to wipe his eyes. He had all he could do from breaking down.

Michael took advantage of the slight pause to add a few words. "Golly, sir, I'm so happy about the promotion, But I, well, you know, sir, I've never done the night shift before. Of course, I'm eager, sir, please don't get me wrong. I'm very eager. And if you think I can do it, I'll do it. I'll do my very best."

"That's the spirit, Michael; that's the spirit I'm looking for. And, oh, by the way, Timothy'll be in charge. He's a year older, so that gives him some seniority, if you know what I mean. You'll be the assistant manager under him."

Assistant manager, and at nineteen—he could hardly believe it. How proud they'd be at home when they heard about it! He was overwhelmed. "Yes, sir, of course. Anything you say, sir. That's fine with me."

"Good, very good! OK; you start next Sunday night, at twelve sharp. Timothy has the keys. He knows what has to be done. Do whatever he says. Then everything will work out fine. OK?"

"Yes, sir, all OK."

The store was a good hour's drive from home but, even so, he wanted to be early, especially on the first night. And so, early he was, arriving at 11:15 in the evening. No one was there yet, so he spent the time walking around near the building. Then, at 11:30, a sharp-looking Mustang convertible pulled up with Timothy at the wheel. Beside him was a young blond, heavily made up with mascara (eyebrows and eyelashes) rouge (for the cheeks), and purple cosmetic paste (for the lips). Seeing him, she waved as if they had been friends for a lifetime. In the back seat was another woman wearing huge glasses and stretching her neck to see who it was standing in front of the store.

"Michael, good to see you" Get in! We'll take a little spin."

"But, is there time? I mean," glancing at his watch, "we've only got half an hour."

"Plenty of time! Plenty of time! Don't worry! We'll have a little drink first before getting down to business. Besides, I've been telling the girls about you. They're dying to meet you."

The door swung open and the girl in front pulled her seat forward so that he could enter the back. Presently, he found himself sitting next to the inquisitive girl similarly painted and wearing enormous red, white and blue earrings. She had a habit of waving her arms whenever she spoke and, at each wave, a puff of Michel Germain deodorant wafted through the air, almost choking him. The car swung rapidly in a half-circle and sped off down the highway towards Stroudsburg. A few minutes later, they pulled up to a small pub tucked in behind some shrubbery. A pink light hanging from a tree threw a bit of light on a sign on the front door:

"Dance Hall in Basement. No Dogs Allowed. Pay as You Enter."

"Well," said Timothy, "here we are! We'll loosen up a bit with a few quickies."

Having made their way down a curling staircase, they found an empty booth. (Even at this hour, the place was crowded.) Once seated, the girls began to page through a list of songs on the juke box at the side of the table. Timothy handed them a few quarters and shortly afterwards, the music started: Hank Williams, "Your Cheating Heart"; Kenny Rogers, "Ruby, Don't Take Your Love to Town," and the like. Shortly after having ordered, a waitress arrived with their drinks: beer for Timothy and the girls, a Pepsi for Michael. A few minutes later, Timothy took the hand of the tall girl, stepped up to the floor, and began to dance. Michael was left with the patriotic girl.

"Hope ya don' min' me asking," she said, "How old are you?"

"Nineteen."

"Nineteen! You're just a kid. Where da' ya live?"

"Dunmore."

"Dunmore! Where's that?"

"Near Scranton."

"Scranton! That's far."

"Yes, a bit, but I don't mind the drive."

"Is that so? Even at night?" After a big gulp, the questions continued. "Wha' da ya do for a living, if I may ask? Just work? Must be boring."

Sensing that she had been drinking earlier, and not sure if she could handle long sentences, he tried to make his answers as short as possible. "I'm a student."

"Ya don' say. Wha' da ya study?"

"Theology."

"Technology? Ya wanna be a carpenter?"

He smiled, without answering. He knew more was coming. It was.

"Where'd ya say you lived?"

OK, let her have it. "Duxbury, Massachusetts."

"Masschewits? Where's that?"

"Oh, up north."

"Why da ya live there?"

"I'm a seminarian. I live at a seminary there."

"A cemetery! Hah! Thas' a good one! You a ghost or somethin'? Tell me another one."

Thank God, just around that time Timothy and his friend came back to the table.

"OK, Michael. I just talked to Roger. He'll take the girls home. We'd better shove off."

They reached the store in a few minutes. It was 1:15.

Once inside, Timothy gave directions.

"OK, this is how it is. You take the first break. I'll wake you at two; then it's my turn."

"Huh? The first break?"

"Right! There's nothing to do yet—just load the stuff on the shelves. The real work starts when they bring the bread and stuff, so we've got the whole night. Beside, you must be tired coming all the way from Dunmore. But, wait here. First things first."

He was back in a minute, carrying a large bag, which he emptied on a box: a large cream cheese cake, a bucket of ice cream, some chocolate syrup, a bag of peanuts, several bars of Snickers and two large bottles of Coke. Party time.

With everything deliciously consumed, it didn't take Michael long to doze off, the couch in the back room being soft and everything very quiet. But the next thing he knew, someone was shaking his shoulder. "Michael, get up! It's time." He opened his eyes to see Timothy standing over him. It was 2:15. A few minutes later, Timothy was fast asleep.

At 3:00 o'clock, Timothy was in such a deep sleep, it seemed a pity to wake him, and so he decided to let him sleep a bit longer. After all, the trucks hadn't arrived yet. After another hour passed, he tapped Timothy's shoulder.

"Timothy, wake up! It's time!"

Timothy struggled to his feet and glanced wearily at his watch. "Four o'clock. *Four o'clock*! Oh, my God! We haven't loaded half of the stuff on the shelves!"

The scene would have made a good movie. They looked like robots, frantically shoving cans, sacks of sugar and salt—whatever—onto the shelves. Some of the labels faced backwards, others were upside down. Bottles of pickles stood next to bottles of olives, and bottles of olives next to jars of peanut butter. It didn't matter. Get the stuff up there . . . pronto! And then—Oh, God!— here came the trucks! Big trucks, little trucks, long trucks, short trucks, bread trucks, dairy trucks, meat trucks, vegetable trucks—oh, oh, oh!—all coming at the same time. Rush, rush! Quick, quick! No time, no time! Oh, Jesus! Oh, Mary! Oh, Boss!

How the two of them managed to stack the shelves, empty the trucks full of bread, cakes, meat, vegetables, and fruit, and get everything in place, and do the same with the milk, butter, cheese, yogurt, salad, and ice cream is anyone's guess. But somehow or other they did it. Good thing! At exactly 7:45 a.m., a white Chevrolet van pulled up in front of the store. He entered the story with a smile, which widened considerably when he saw that everything was in perfect order.

"Timothy, Michael, I want you to know," he said, as his chest expanded, "I want you to know how proud I am of you, absolutely proud. Here it is your first night on the job and you did everything perfectly. Perfectly! Why, look at you, sweating like that! I know, I know the story; you don't have to explain. You worked so hard all night, it just broke out in a sweat. What a team! What a team!"

Michael didn't say a word. (He couldn't, shaking as he was like a leaf.) He let Timothy do the talking.

"Thank you, sir, thank you very much. It was nothing really, nothing at all. Yes, I have to admit, it was quite a struggle to get everything in place, but we did it. We did it, sir, all for the honor and glory of the good old A&P."

"That's right, that's the spirit! Wonderful! But, well, looks like you two could use a good rest before you come back again tonight. Do the same as you did tonight. Don't change a thing. What a team! Bravo! Bravo!"

P.S. Would someone drive by the area (along route 611, near Stroudsburg), they wouldn't find the grocery story there anymore. The place has been taken over by a toy company, Toys R Us. (Was that fate?) The building has been repainted and the front windows replaced with larger ones. But it's hard to erase some of the memories of the former place, even though it happened so many years ago—memories that, even now, bring out a bit of laughter. Hurrah for the good old days! Hurrah for the good old A&P! Hurrah! Hurrah! Hurrah!

THE MAIL MUST
GO THROUGH

"It's wonderful to have you home. We've been waiting every day."

"Thanks, Mom! I was lucky to get away. Ah! Three weeks free . . . no classes . . . no meetings . . . no deadlines . . . God is good!"

"Yes. You can have a little rest now." (Pause) "Oh, I almost forgot. Can you see Mr. Byron? He wants you to see him right away. Sounds urgent."

"Mr. Byron?" (Pause) "Oh, God!"

"What's the matter? Is something wrong?"

"No, I mean, I just remembered. Before I left last summer, he talked about needing some help at Christmas. Everybody did, but his place was the farthest one away and harder to find people. Oh, God! I completely forgot!"

"Well, just see what he has in mind. Maybe it's something else."

The house was always the same: Grand Central Station! When he entered the living room, Mr. Byron was sitting at one end of a sofa holding a baby in one arm, puffing a pipe and, somehow or other, still managing to glance at a newspaper. Ms. Byron was at the other end with a baby (another one, slightly older) — nursing her, and yelling constantly. "Timothy, give Jeffrey some of your marbles! You have enough! Sarah, take Angie to the toilet, and this time be sure she gets on *top* of the seat! Beth, give Alex a carrot! He shouldn't chew on the table like that!" Three other children were putting a puzzle together, while two others were playing with a kitten.

As soon as he entered, Mr. Byron held out his hand, and motioned for him to sit. They soon got down to business.

"Father Michael, welcome home! It's good to see you! But, listen, I'm desperate." Briggs pulled out two days ago. Said he fell off a ladder. Jones has bronchitis, and Wilson suddenly decided to go ice fishing. Ice fishing! Can you imagine! So, that's it! I'm desperate. Can you do it? I'm really desperate.

"Well, I . . ."

"It's only four days: tomorrow till Thursday."

"But . . . well, you know, I've never done that kind of thing before. And I don't know the west side so well . . ."

"No problem! No problem at all! We're sorting out everything: names, streets, codes. Just follow the numbers. No problem at all! Oh, by the way, you'll get a bundle. The post office isn't stingy at Christmas."

There was a long pause. You could almost hear Mr. Byron mumbling a prayer. Maybe that did it. "OK. It's only a few days. I'll do it."

"Terrific! That's the spirit! OK, we start tomorrow. Leave at five-thirty. Dress warmly! Gloves, a good hat, boots, scarf, long johns . . . Just imagine you're in Alaska with the polar bears and the Eskimos. Ha, ha!" (When he laughed, the baby suddenly looked up, smiled, and reached for the pipe. Mr. Byron turned his face to the side, and the baby went back to sucking his thumb.)

Breakfast was ready: hot pancakes, with all the accouterments: butter, molasses, strawberries, whipped cream, and coffee on the side. Her son might freeze to death, but at least he wouldn't starve! She kissed him as he made his way to the door. He felt ready for anything.

The car took some time to start—not surprising at ten degrees below zero—but then, suddenly, the engine jumped to life. Mr. Byron cleared some snow from the windows and, after a few minutes, off they went, like hearty Mormons, to the wild, wild west.

Already at six-fifteen, the room was full. The mailmen in the group were tugging at mailbags, sorting and filing mail, and shouting directions. Others—part-timers like himself, he supposed—although dressed in a motley assortment of heavy coats, ear muffins, hats and boots, were crowding around a potbelly stove trying to keep the blood circulating.

A few minutes elapsed when, presently, Mr. Byron emerged from his office, cleared his throat and, moving to the center of the room, said in a loud voice: "Now, then . . ." Everyone stopped what they were doing and focused their attention.

"Good morning, everybody! It's good to see you all, and thank you very much for coming. Sorry about the time—quite early, isn't it?—and sorry about the weather. Seems like it snowed all night, with more to come today. A typical Pennsylvania Christmas.

OK, men! Now we've got a big job ahead of us . . . piles of letters and cards . . . packages . . . a few boxes. Well, that's the way it should be. People love each other, and our job is to see that all this love that's going around reaches the right places. So, that's it: the mail must go through, and you, my dear fellows, are the ones who'll get it through.

Now, before we start, there are just a few little rules, not too many, but they're important, so listen carefully. First, watch out for the dogs! Try to ignore them — absolutely! But if they cause any trouble, well, you've all got your key chains. If worse comes to worse, use them! If that doesn't work, use your feet! Kick his snout, belly, arse . . . whatever you feel is appropriate under the given circumstances. Don't worry about getting sued. You're merely acting in a defensive manner. And if need be, Uncle Sam will back you up to the last penny. Do you understand my meaning? (He pauses to clear his throat.) OK, good. Next: don't talk to any strangers. If somebody comes up to have a chat, just wave 'em off—with a smile, of course—and keep going. Everybody loves a mailman . . . we bring good news, but some fellows out there are looking for a handout, or maybe a little extra money that might be inside some of those letters. So just keep walking! Pay no attention! Am I understood? (When no one answers, he continues.) Good! Finally, don't go around visiting people! There are a lot of nice folks out there, and I realize that you may know some of them; maybe some are your relatives. But, gentlemen, this isn't tea time. It's time to deliver the mail. So please resist. You're not Santa Claus; you're mailmen. And the important thing is—and I hope you always keep this in mind—the mail must go through! (He pauses for a moment.) All right, any questions? (When there are no questions, he continues.) Good! Now just step up here to the window, give you name, and get your bundle and keys.

Good luck, and see you all back here by —he glances at his watch—one o'clock."

A kind of confused scrambling went on for a few minutes, as people buttoned up, sorted their belongings, and lined up before the window. A few were asking questions about where, exactly, their route started, but eventually the room began to empty. Michael gave his name and was given a large, heavy bag packed full. He checked his map again, shouldered the bag, and made his way outside.

Fortunately, the first house was only a few blocks away from the post office. And, just as fortunately, the first few addresses were written in legible handwriting: Mr. and Ms. Henry Adamson, 102 St. Anne's Street, Scranton, Pennsylvania. The only trouble was, he couldn't wear the gloves! Try as he may, it was simply too difficult to sort out the letters with the gloves on. Therefore, he decided that, come what may, he'd only wear a glove on his left hand, the one carrying the mail. When the right hand became numb, he'd warm it between his crotch. In any event—right!—the mail must go through!

Most of the homes along the route were quiet, as if the people inside were still asleep. But now and then, someone would peep out through a window, or meet him at the front door with a smile. Presently, somewhere around the middle of the third block, he saw an elderly man, all smiles and rubbing his hands furiously, standing outside on the porch.

"Ah! Good to see you, lad! Good to see you! Glad tidings for us, is it? Well, well, bless your soul!" The man turned the letters over and over several times, as if he couldn't believe he'd received so many at one time. Two of the letters bore large, colorful stamps from another country.

"Ah, praise the Lord! From me sister in Cork, is it? And this one, from Sligo! La-di-da! Bless their lovin' hearts! Bless them! Bless them!"

Then, glancing up suddenly, the man gestured with his hand. "My God, lad! Look at your hands! And your face! You're half frozen, you are! Come in! Come in! You've got to warm yourself a bit over the fire!"

"Oh, no, no! Thank you, thank you very much, but, you see, I can't do it! I'd like to, but . . . sorry!"

"But, laddie, it tisn't a visit, is it! Just a wee bit of a . . . how do you say it? . . . a pause; that's it, a pause along the road of life. Yes, that's what it is: a pause along the road of life! Besides; it's for your health . . . for your health, mind you — to warm the bones, not to mention the heart. So, come in, laddie, come in, just for a wee bit! Warm yourself up, for heaven's sake! You'll do a better job once you're inside a spell, believe me. At least, come inside the door! Come, laddie, come!" The man held the door wide open with one hand, the other coaxing persuasively, as if he wouldn't take no for an answer.

The words registered quickly, "just a wee bit . . . warm yourself up . . . do a better job once you're inside a spell." And, actually, come to think of it, it really wasn't a visit, was it? Not like sitting down and chatting over the news, or anything like that. No, no, of course not. He took a quick glance around, and then, quick as a flash, stepped into the vestibule, feeling a bit guilty, to be sure, but which feeling evaporated just as quickly once he felt the warm, comforting air inside.

"Ah, that's better, much better, isn't it, laddie?" No sooner was this said than an elderly woman entered the hallway carrying a tray on which were three very large, very full glasses of very red wine.

"Oh, just as I thought! It's the mailman! I knew it right away . . . heard you from the kitchen. Imagine! Poor dear . . . trudging the streets all alone on such a freezing day and with such a heavy load. My, my! Now, come! Come and have a wee little sip! Port, it is. And a new bottle opened just for you."

"Well," said the mailman, "well, that is, really, I, I appreciate it, I mean, your kindness. But, you see, well, I, I mean, the mail . . . "

"Yes, yes, I know. Now, come, laddie, not another word! 'Tis a form of medicine, it 'tis—medicine to warm the heart. 'Warm the heart'—that's what me father would say—'and the rest will take care of itself.'"

The man held up his glass. "To your health, laddie, and to the health of me good sister in Cork, who always remembers her dear brother in the faraway country. And to me wife's family, too, in Sligo, the family who never lets a day pass without . . ."

The woman smiled and gently lifted her glass. At this, the man, without further ado, straightened up. "Cheers!" he said, "and may all your roads run straight ahead, however bumpy they may be!"

With that, the glasses tipped upwards, froze in midair, then down and inside ran the dark, rich, tingling, so warm, so delicious, so soothing red, red wine.

Outside again, the taste of the wine and the friendliness of the elderly couple simply obliterated any thoughts of the cold. In fact, he walked along now with a kind of sprint in his legs, so much so that all of a sudden the thought ran through his head: how about a bit of a dance right here and now? Hah! That'd wake them up! But, no, that wouldn't do, of course. After all, there was the matter of propriety and, oh, yes, the mail: the mail must go through. In any event, the thought crossed his mind why he hadn't given the whole idea of peddling mail a much better review.

Just as the map indicated, the next mailbox stood at attention there on the corner and, wouldn't you know, right around the time he had managed to empty his sack of the first bundle. Thank the Lord, this one was lighter and, as he started out again, he was sure that he could finish within another two hours or so. That would get him back to the post office right around one. Pretty good timing!

One of the houses in the next section intrigued him: it was painted entirely in bright red, with yellow trimming, for which reason it stood out among all the other houses lining both sides of the street. A new Harley-Davidson stood in the driveway and, behind it, a sky-blue Porsche. He was also surprised by the fact that there were a good seven items just for this one place: five letters and two small packages.

As he approached the house, he noticed someone looking down at him from an upstairs window. Then, just as he was about to put the mail through the slit in the door, it suddenly opened. A woman, somewhere in her late fifties, scanned him up and down, as if she couldn't contain her disbelief.

"Oh, my Lord! Look at you! Just look! Oh, it's too much . . . too much for words"!

Not quite sure what the woman was talking about, the mailman smiled awkwardly, then, as if to divert attention—both hers and his own—he suddenly shoved the mail at her. Not in the least deterred, the woman continued.

"Oh, how utterly *devastating*, so, so . . . *crippling*! Why look at you! You look like, like a penguin . . . no, no, like a polar bear, like the Iceman! It's so devastating! *Devastating*!"

Again, he was taken aback, even less sure how to react than with the Irishman. Strangely enough, the image of himself hanging in midair one day years ago when he tried to pole vault over Roaring Brook—not sure whether he'd be able to get back to the place from where he had pushed off, make it across to the other side, or wind up with a good dunking in the river—darted across his mind.

"My child!" the woman continued, "you're absolutely frozen. How can you bear it? Oh, it's so, so . . . [he could see it coming] *devastating*! You must come in! You must come in! How can you be so cruel to yourself, so, so . . . *masochistic?* Oh, oh, it's too much for words!"

Figuring he was beginning to get her character into better focus, the mailman's confidence returned (a bit). "Thank you, ma'm," he said. "I really appreciate it, really do. But, you see, I have a route to follow. And there's a schedule. And still a lot of houses to go. And, you know, all those dogs along the way . . . Well, what I mean is, you see, there's isn't much time, I mean, with all these letters and . . . and everything. What?" He pointed weakly to the half-empty bag.

"Rubbish!" said the woman, "utter rubbish! (Bye-bye confidence.) "Young man, I am fully aware of the situation. And let me tell you something: the more worthwhile the goal, the more it requires proportionate effort. But who can carry on the work when the worker is immobilized by frostbite, overwhelmed by the tonnage of that which must be born, and incapacitated by the distance to be traversed. It's just, too, too *devastating*!"

A little squeak was all he could manage: "Huh?"

"And so, my child, I leave you no other choice: drop that bag and enter this house . . . NOW!"

Before he could say Jack Robinson, down went the bag. Marching into the parlor, he was tempted to salute but, for some reason or other, desisted. After all, he had to salvage some honor.

"All right," said the hostess. "Now what is it? Campari, Irish Whiskey, or Vodka Martini? I suppose there's still some Rum left, if you prefer, or Courvoisier. Forget the Sour Mash. I finished it off in the bath last night. Well?"

For the life of him, he couldn't remember a word of what she had said. "I'll . . . I'll have the Whiskey Irish" he blurted . . . "on ice, lots of ice." A moment later, he wondered why he'd asked for ice.

"Martha! Maaartha! Two Irish Whiskeys . . . with lots of ice, thank you. And mach schnell! He doesn't have all day."

She motioned him to sit. "You know," she went on, "you remind me of Tom. You wouldn't know him, of course. He's a bit older than you. One of my best students."

"You, you were a teacher"?

"Yes, most of the time, anyway, that is, except for the time I wasn't. Ha, ha!"

"Ha, ha!" he also laughed, not sure whether the wine he had drunk a short time earlier had already blotted out half of his perception, or whether some ice had lodged inside his ears and he wasn't hearing correctly.

After the whiskey had arrived, and having taken a few sips, he felt himself becoming bolder, so much so that he decided to take the offensive. "And where did you teach?" he asked. Tierra del Fuego popped up in his mind.

"Oh, here and there. The Sorbonne threw me out when I told them Descartes was an idiot. Imagine! *Cogito, ergo sum*. Did you ever hear such bullshit! As if man were the measure of the universe! I tried Balliol for a while, but they couldn't stomach what I said about Hegel. Another imbecile! Can you imagine stuffing everything into syntheses and antitheses? What crap! Obviously they'd never heard of Spinoza."

Huh? Descartes . . . Hegel . . . who? what? The whiskey was taking its toll.

"Well, well, well! Looks like you're running dry. How about another, just for the road?"

Having finished the second drink, he tried to stand, but fell back onto the sofa. On the second effort he did much better, though, once on his feet, he wondered why the far side of the room was tilting so much to the right. "Shanks, shanks again," he said, dimly aware that the words weren't coming out quite as he'd like. "I shink it's enough. And there's shis job to do. So, shanks from my heart. Good-bye and good luck!"

The woman led him to the door. "Are you all right? I mean, those two whiskeys . . . You drank them rather quickly, didn't you? *Devastating! Too devastating!"*

"Yes, yes, I'm fine, jus' fine. And, believe me, madam, I truly appreciate your kindness. Truly I do. If you're ever around the post office, drop in to visit. Jus' tell Mr. Byron that you sent me."

For the first time in his life, he felt that going down stairs could be much more difficult than going up but, be as it may, he managed to reach the bottom—barely— without falling. Ah, he thought, God is good, so good!

For some reason or other, from then on, the numbers and names on the letters seemed to be written in Chinese. He couldn't figure out why. Was someone playing tricks, testing his eyesight, or whether he really had finished graduate school? But, darned if they'd succeed. He had a job to do and, by God, he'd do it . . . right down to the (hic) last letter.

Had someone paid close attention on that particular day—the day before Christmas—to the lone figure making his way down the street a block away from the post office, he would have observed the curious figure of a young man crossing and recrossing the street with a bit of an unsteady gait and an ever lighter bag of mail. There was a twinkle in his eye as he went along and, for some reason or other, each of the homes on the block seemed to be favored with a rather large amount of mail. Undoubtedly, some of it found its way to the wrong house, for by this time the mailman's eyes seemed to have become a bit blurred—the result, no doubt, of the steady snowfall—with the result that Ms. Jones's mail found its ways into Mr. Anthony O'Connor's mailbox, and Mr. O'Connor's into that of Mr. Watanabe's. (Hopefully, they'd sort it out afterwards.)

[The story continues one year later.]

"It's so good to have you home again!"

"Yes, I was lucky. It's the first time I've ever been able to have consecutive Christmas vacations. Isn't it great! (He pauses for a while.) Oh, by the way, does Mr. Byron know I'm home?"

"Yes, I told him that you'd be here for the holidays."

"Did he say anything about the mail, I mean, anything about needing someone?"

"No, he never mentioned it. Curious, isn't it? I know he needs people. Ms. Byron told me that, like last year, somebody suddenly couldn't make it, so they're short of personnel."

"Oh, really?"

"Yes, but that's all she said. Funny, isn't it? Here we are right next door. And it'd be simple to go there with Mr. Byron. The pay was very good, wasn't it?"

"Yes, very good! Made it worthwhile, I mean, despite the snow and all."

"Hum . . . I wonder why he hasn't called."

"Ah, yes—makes one wonder, doesn't it?"

Passport, Please!

"Ah, excuse me, sir! Would you mind moving to the line over there?"

"Oh, yes, sure, sure thing!" The man moves one line over to the right, bowing and smiling all the time, while trying to remember what kind of documents he might need next and why on earth, though he'd been throughout the whole procedure zillions of times, he can never remember these things. About fifteen minutes later, he moves ahead (finally) to the line immediately in front of the customs officer's booth. The smile has slowly faded away and the shoulders have drooped a bit but, somewhat like Napoleon at Waterloo, he has determined to put up a good front and stick it out to the end.

"Passport, please!"

He pulls out his passport from his shirt pocket and hands it to the customs officer. The smile has been turned on again, a bit forced this time, but backed up by his intention to abide by all the laws and rules of the country.

"Let's see now . . . It says here that you live here in Japan. And you're a teacher. All right! So, everything looks good, right in order. Hum! Lots of stamps, eh? Looks like you travel a lot, Mr. White. Business? Volunteering? Adventures of one kind or another?"

The tone of voice was pleasant, encouraging a just-as-pleasant response. "Yes, you might say that" (whatever "that" might mean). I go a lot to the Philippines. Volunteer work . . . visiting friends . . . things like that."

"I see. Well, everything looks fine. No problems. Now, for the next part. If you don't mind, I'd like to ask you a few questions."

"A few questions? What kind of questions?"

"Oh, just simple things . . . nothing too difficult. Any kindergarten child can handle them. Just relax, put on your thinking cap for a few minutes, and you'll fly right through. Now, then, are you ready?"

"Yes, I guess so."

"All right. Now for the first question. "Where do koalas mate, in trees or on the ground?"

"Huh?"

"Now, don't worry. Just relax. I'll repeat the question. Take your time. We've got plenty . . . [he glances at the crowd of people waiting their turn] . . . ah, that is, try your best and leave the rest to . . . ah, to me."

Mr. White, trying to figure out how to answer the question, puts his hand to his chin, then scratches his head. His eyes roll up a bit, then his mouth forms into a pucker.

"Gee!" he responds, "that's a tough one. I . . . I, well, that is, to tell the truth, I'm sorry, but I haven't the slightest idea where they mate."

"Bravo, Mr. White! Bravo! That's the answer! That's the perfect answer! As you know, those little buggers are so foxy, nobody know when or where they do it. And they do it all the time: daytime . . . nighttime . . . all the time . . . anywhere, everywhere . . . Mr. White, I must congratulate you. You know, you're one of the few who gets that one right. It's one of the toughest questions in the book."

The man pauses, then lowers his head a bit as he flips through the book again.

"Oh, here! Here's another one! Don't worry, this one looks easier. Here you go! Ready? "Do you love the Emperor?"

"What? What's that?"

"O.K., I'll repeat it slowly: 'Do . . . you . . . love . . . the . . . Emperor?'"

"Do you mean the Emperor of Japan?"

"Oh, now, Mr. White, I would expect much more of you, much more. I'm not talking about the Emperor of Mongolia. I'm talking about the Emperor of Japan . . . *Japan*! . . . here, in this country. OK, let me put the question to you once again. "'Do you love the Emperor of . . . [he puts special emphasis on the last word] *Japan*?'"

The smile becomes visible again. "You mean the fellow who waves to all the people on New Year's Day from up there on the balcony?"

"Yes, yes, that's the one. Good! Good! Go on, go on!"

"The one who likes sumo?"

"Yes, yes, that's the one. Good . . . good! Keep going . . . keep going!"

"The one who smells the gladiolas and . . . and who feeds the ducks in the pond out there?"

"Yes, yes! Absolutely brilliant, Mr. White! Absolutely brilliant!"

(There's a pause—a very long pause.) "Ah, er . . . excuse me. Can you repeat the question again?"

"Oh, Mr. White! Oh! And here I thought . . ."

"Yes, I do! I love him! I LOVE him! . . . absolutely . . . with all my heart!"

"Oh, Mr. White, I knew you could do it! I knew it all the time!" (There's another pause as the officer sifts through the book.) "And now for the last question. But, first, some advice. This is the most important question of all. Answer it right and you're IN. Answer it wrong and you're . . . well, thank you for stopping by. OK? Do you understand? Do you understand me, Mr. White?"

"Yes, I understand, I understand. I'm ready, very ready. Let's have the question!"

"Good! That's the spirit! OK, here it is." (He straightens up and reads the question slowly, but with strong emphasis on certain words.) 'When Joe Louis met Max Schmeling in their second bout, Louis hit him with a combination of punches that landed Schmeling smack on the canvas. When it was almost all over, the referee bent over and asked Schmeling, 'OK, Max, what's the beef? Lay it on the line! Wha' da ya wanna do?'" OK. Here's the question: "What did Schmeling answer? What did he say to the referee?"

"Wha . . . what did Schmeling say to the referee?" (He rubs his chin again, scratches his head, puckers up his lips, and frowns.) "Gee, that's a tough one, too. Really tough. I . . . I, that is to say, I haven't the slightest idea . . . not the slightest. I'm sorry, but I give up."

"Mister White, Mister White! I knew you could do it! That's perfect! That's the perfect answer! That's just what he said: 'I give up! I give up!' You're a genius, Mr. White, a real genius."

"Well, er, yeah! Right! Sooo . . . can I go through now? Is everything OK?"

"Oh, no, Mr. White! No, no. We can't rush these things, no way! No . . . We still have a few more steps to go through."

"A few more steps?"

"Yes, well, I hope you know, Mr. White, we have a new system here. Just started a few years ago. Nothing bothersome, of course. Just a little, well, let's say a bit of a tick in the system, if you know what I mean."

He wasn't quite sure what the "tick" referred to, but then a quick flash passed through his mind about an article he'd read some time ago in the newspaper—something about fingerprinting to validate all the credentials.

"Oh well, no problem. Whatever . . ."

"Good, that's the spirit. That's what I like. Then we can finish in a jiffy. Now, Mr. White, if you would just put your two fingers down there on the pad. Nothing difficult, you see. Just a matter of procedure. Don't have to press too hard. You know how sensitive these little gadgets are."

"Well, OK." He puts two fingers on the pad. At that, the officer frowns.

"No, Mr. White, not your pinkies! Your *index* fingers. That's what I want: your *index* fingers. (He holds up his two index fingers to demonstrate.) "OK, let's try again."

Once more, the fingers go up, then down on the pad. This time, everything is satisfactory.

"Good, good! Now, let's see. Oh, yes, the photo. OK, Mr. White, how about looking at the camera here— right in the middle? And let's have a nice smile, OK? That's it! That's it, OK! Now, say 'cheese.'"

He manages a smile and the camera does its thing.

"Great! Just great! And now . . . oh, oh, ooooh!"

"What's the matter? Are you OK? Is anything wrong?"

"No, no, not with you. But, you see, with all these rules about fingerprints and stuff, I . . . I just get so nervous, it gives me . . . [he whispers] the *runs*."

"Oh! Really?"

"Yes, really! And right now I've got to *run*."

"Pee pee?"

"No, much worse: pooh pooh."

"Oh, pooh pooh. That's bad; that's really bad!"

"Yes, Mr. White. And look at all those people there! But (he pauses for a second) . . . hey, listen! I just got an idea. Can you step in here for a minute? The door's over there on the left."

When he hears what the officer has in mind, he's very surprised. "*I* do it? You want *me* to do it?"

"That's right. Listen, it'll only take a minute. I'll be back in a jiffy. Toilet's on the other side. Here, take this badge! Nobody'll notice. Oh, the cap! Take the cap, too!" He leans over and puts the cap on Mr. White's head. (It's a little too small, but anyway . . .) Then he pins a badge on his jacket. That done, he opens the door and begins walking quickly in the opposite direction.

"But . . . wait! Wait! What am I supposed to do?"

The officer stops for a moment and calls back: "Don't worry! Do what I did to you. And don't forget the stamp! See you in a minute!"

Mr. White enters the booth, adjusts himself in the seat and, feeling like king of the jungle, looks out over the crowd. "Next!" he calls out in a loud voice, and a gentleman comes forward.

About fifteen minutes later, the customs officer returns. When they meet, he gingerly takes back his cap and badge and once again takes his seat inside the booth.

"Thanks, Mr. White, thanks a lot! You saved the day." (He pauses as he looks out at the empty lobby.) "Hey, where is everybody? Where'd they all go?"

Mr. White smiles broadly. "Well, you see, it wasn't hard at all, once you get the knack of it. Photo . . . stamp. . . . 'next'! Photo . . . stamp . . . 'next'! Not hard at all!"

The officer grins. "Listen, Mr. White! (He bends over and speaks in a low voice.) Can you keep a secret—just between the two of us?"

"Sure, you know me."

"Well, actually, I think these new rules, you know, the ones about the fingerprinting and stuff . . . Well, don't tell anybody, but I think it's for the birds. The old way of checking just the passports worked just fine. And we didn't have all these lines. But, anyway, Mr. White, thanks a million. You've made my day!"

"You've made mine, too. Bye!"

THE ENTRANCE EXAM

Slightly bent and carrying a cane, a tall, impeccably dressed gentleman (undoubtedly a distinguished professor) enters the room at the strike of the bell. Somewhat like a fountain gushing water, a mass of white hair springs from the top of his head, spills over the sides of his face, flows downwards and settles into a full beard stretching several inches below his chin. He carries a bundle of papers in one hand while, with the other, pokes tappingly along until he reaches the front desk. Having deposited the papers on the desk, he removes his glasses and begins to wipe off a thin mist with his handkerchief. Were someone to remember his behavior some years ago, they would have been astounded by the way he could remember long passages of *Paradise Lost* and *The Waste Land*. But that was years ago. Now he had all he could do to remember his phone number. Nevertheless, there was still the voice. Ah, yes, the voice—one that could instill fear in the hearts of freshmen who failed to hand in their homework on time or who habitually came late. Yes, the voice—still strong and clear—was the one thing that continued to melt steel. And now that he had a captive audience of nervous students sitting for an entrance exam, his intention was to give another performance to show again that he was still someone to be reckoned with. That said, he raised his head and shouted with all the force he could muster: "Ladies and gentlemen! Attention, please!" It worked, indeed, worked so well that four or five of the students sitting in the front row suddenly jerked their heads upwards, daring not even to wink. All eyes now focused on the powerful voice compelling their attention. He has succeeded. Good! What next? Oh, yes, how to continue? OK, he's got it. As if mesmerized by something stuck on the back wall, he stares straight ahead, managing to avoid looking at any of students of whom, it might be added, he is deathly afraid of.

"Ladies and gentlemen!" he repeats. "May I have your attention, your undivided attention? (Pause) "My name is Professor I. Kan Tinkle." (He now inhales deeply to fill his lungs with more (hot) air.) "You are here to take an examination. And I am here to, ah, ah, to administer it . . . to administer it in the name of the faculty of Picklepecker University, Nagoya, Japan. Undoubtedly, you are fully aware of the importance of this examination. Therefore, I need not tell you that your future life, the future of the country, in fact, the future of the world depends on it. Some of you will swim, some will sink, and some of you, I suppose, will squeeze through by the skin of your teeth." (He pauses again to take another deep breath as well as to try to remember the rest of his speech that he has given for the past forty years without a single variation.) "Do some of you want to become doctors?" (Another pause.) "Engineers . . . teachers . . . lawyers . . . astronauts? Well, it all depends on how well you do in this examination which, needless to say, will separate the men from the mice." Suddenly noticing that most of the students are females, he quickly corrects himself. "That is to say, er, the adults from the children. After all . . ." Just as he is beginning to feel in complete control of the situation, another gentleman, much younger, sidles ever so carefully up to the front desk and, as discreetly as possible, extends his arm showing the professor his watch. The elderly professor (wisely) decides that enough has been said for the moment. Then, turning to his compatriot, he adds a few more final words. "Ah, let me introduce my colleague, a distant relative, Assistant Professor I. Kan Tinkletoo." Having said this, although completely at variance with the image he has been trying to impose, he then bursts out in a high-pitched giggle, letting out what might best be described as the shriek of a mad hyena: "He, he, he, he, he!" A few of the student look at each other, some smiling, a few giggling. The professor then turns to his assistant. "Ah, now there, Mr. Tinkletoo, would you like to say a few words to the examinees before they begin?"

The assistant suddenly puts his hand to his chest and blurts out, "Who, me?"

"Yes, yes, say a few words of encouragement to the students. I'm sure they'd appreciate it."

With this, the professor sits down, rubs his glasses again and, within the space of about thirty seconds, drops his head and falls asleep.

Caught off guard by the sudden request, and without the slightest idea of what to say, the assistant begins to talk in a rapid voice. "Ah, well, ah . . . all I wanna say is, heads up! That's about it! Oh, and, ah, good luck, good luck! You'll need it! I mean, you wouldn't believe it: I mean, we're sinking fast! No kidding! That's why we've got this new pool. Unbelievable! Even has a sauna! But, lemme tell you, if the numbers go down any more, forget it! Kaput! Know what I mean? And you know what'll happen then? People like me'll be feeding the birds! And besides . . ."

Just then, the professor, having completed his nap, raises his hand. "Ah, thank you, thank you for such an inspiring speech! But (looking at his watch), it seems like time has arrived. And so, dear assistant, on behalf of our noble colleagues and the esteemed administration of Picklepecker University, I hereby order you: Distribute the examinations!"

Having said this, the assistant moves up and down the aisles passing out question-and-answer sheets—quite a job, since all kinds of bags, lunch boxes, textbooks, tennis rackets, baseball bats, and other items clutter the aisles. Having managed somehow to accomplish this, he again takes his position at the front of the room. Then he and his assistant simply wait for the sound of the buzzer. A minute later, it sounds. Immediately, eighty-four heads dip close to the papers on their desks and begin to read the preliminary instructions.

Dear students, before you begin to answer the questions given below, please read the following message carefully.

We, the faculty members of Picklepecker University, have decided that long, involved questions are a thing of the past. What is called for nowadays is succinctness, conciseness, compactness, pithiness, terseness, transiency, brevity and simplicity. With this in mind, we have decided to limit the entrance examinations to the minimum, just ten questions. But, dear students, be well advised that, although the examination is short, our accomplished teachers have done extensive research in formulating them, having consulted works in ancient Sumerian codicils, Averroes' influence on scholastic philosophy, the origin of the Archemedian screw, and stuff like that. We threw in a few more questions just for the heck of it. Stay awake, and good luck!

Questions: Please answer the following questions by writing True or False in the blank space. You will have thirty minutes to answer all the questions, so there is no need to rush. If you do not know the answer to a particular question, do not peek at the answers of the students next to you. Just leave a blank and go on to the next question. (But don't leave too many blanks).

1. Mount Fuji is a mountain. (   )

2. A pretty mule looks as good as a horse. (   )

3. Some oranges are yellow. (   )

4. Every dog should be allowed one bite. (   )

5. An old eagle is better than a young crow. (   )

6. Lady de Winter, the wife of Lord de Winter, had a fleur-de-lis tattoo on her right shoulder. No one knows what was on the left one. (   )

7. An egg is meat, since it engenders a chicken. (   )

8. All cats look gray in the dark. (   )

9. Never trust people who smile constantly. They're either selling something or not very bright. (   )

10. Dorothy Parker, noted critic and actress, is also famous for her wit. One of the memorable things she

said was: "When I get up in the morning, the first thing I do is brush my teeth and sharpen my tongue." (   )

This is the end of the examination. Thank you, and take it easy.

A Note to the Reader: Dear Reader, we hope and trust that the following incident will not shock you to any inordinate way, however, since we feel obliged to relate to you all the circumstances involved in this particular entrance examination, and lest there be any misunderstandings, we feel it our duty to report everything that happened during the day just as it took place. This said, let us continue our story.

Now, while all the students were diligently trying to answer the questions, it could not but be noticed by the two proctoring professors that a particular student sitting in the back of the room was grimacing terribly. Obviously, he was the victim of some kind of physical, if not mental, stress. Now and then, the said student would wipe perspiration from his forehead with his handkerchief. At other times, he would suddenly bend over and rub his stomach with both hands. Finally, seemingly unable to bear whatever was distressing him, the student raised his hand. The head professor, noticing this, immediately signaled to the junior professor that he should approach the student to see what was happening. However, when the young professor was halfway down the aisle, the student suddenly sprang from his seat, ran to the door, and rushed out of the room. Once in the hallway, he began yelling at the top of his voice, "Toilet! Toilet! Where's the toilet?" When someone in the hall pointed to a nearby lavatory, the student dashed into the room, found an empty stall, and entered. However, Lady Fortune being elsewhere that day, just as he was in the process of closing the door, there came this terrific blast—enough, surely, to propel a rocket to Mars—from the rear end part of his body. Now, it could be said that this was both good and bad news: good in the sense that the blast managed to free the remains of a heavy meal taken the previous night, thereby resulting in a tremendous sense of relief; bad in the sense that it soiled not only his underwear but his trousers as well. However, he quickly noticed to his great relief that a full roll of toilet paper was waiting his use. While doing his best to clean up the mess, he suddenly became aware of the fact that he had only answered four questions of the exam. *I must go back, he said to himself. I've studied so hard . . . I must go back! But, oh, God, how? Ahhh!* Just then, a flash of inspiration crossed his mind. *"That's it! My shirt! It's long enough. I'll pull it down! That should do it!"*

Having said this, he rolled up his soiled clothes, made his way to the door, and peeked outside. Good! No one was there, neither was anyone in the corridor. Quickly making his way back to the exam room, he quietly opened the door. But, alas! Having surprised many of the students by leaving the room so hurriedly, now, upon reentering, a number of them, seeing him half-naked, stared at him in disbelief. Some of them, boys in particular, burst out laughing. When he sat down, the girl on his left side turned her head and began to look out the window, while another centered her attention on her eraser. Doing his best to focus on the present, he realized that only ten minutes remained before the exam finished. *Pattern*, he thought, *there must be a pattern! If I can only figure out the pattern! Let's see! The first three questions are true. I'm sure that the next three are also true. That's the way they make these tests!* Having beforehand answered the first three questions with Ts, he quickly put Ts on the next three. But then he thought: *Ah, these people are clever! They never make all the questions true! Let's put an F on number seven. Ok, now back to the pattern.* He then put three more Ts on the last three questions. Just as he scratched the last letter on the exam sheet, the buzzer sounded signaling the end of the examination. He had to endure another few minutes of agony while the assistant collected all the papers, by which time a good half of the students in the room were giggling and laughing. But God is good: when most of the students had left the room, only one, a boy, remained. Sensing what may have happened, he approached the student and offered his jacket. "Here," he said, "keep it! I've got another one at home."

A Note to the Reader

On the same day, just before four o'clock in the afternoon, a group of teachers gather on the third floor of the administration building to score the examinations. Six tables fill the room, and the teachers take a seat, six to a table. Accuracy, of course, is important, but so, too, is speed, since everyone is anxious to go home, have supper, and watch the evening news. Thus, work proceeds rapidly, so much so that after two hours, the main work has been accomplished. When the last paper is scored, the teacher in charge calls for attention.

"Thank you, everyone! Thank you very much! You're getting better and better at this, in fact, news is we've just set a record for finishing so quickly. Of course, the new system helped a lot, too. Well, anyway, the computer gave us some details. 732 students took the exam. 730 passed. Amazing, isn't it? However, even so, it seems like it was a rather tough examination. No one managed to answer more than 7 questions correctly. But there was one exception. Student number 62 got all the questions correct. He must be a genius. I certainly hope he decides to enter our university."

Hearing this, Professor Higgins leans close to Assistant Professor I. Kan Tinkletoo. "Isn't that the one from your room?" "Yes, that right! Number 62. He was sitting in the back row. Something happened during the test—I couldn't figure it out. Halfway through the exam, he suddenly ran out of the room. It's amazing, I mean, after he came back, he was wearing just his shirt. I couldn't figure that out either. Anyway, as soon as he came back, he sat down and started to check the answers off like crazy. Amazing! I mean, the concentration! Unbelievable! Utterly unbelievable!"

THIS IS A PEN

"Akiko?"

"Here!"

"Yoshiaki?"

"Here!"

"Ippei?"

"Ear!"

(Pause) "Ippei, this is an *ear*!" (He points to his ear.)
"Say, 'he, he, he'"!

"He, he, he!" (Everyone laughs.)

"OK. Now say, *hear*."

Finally, getting the pronunciation right, he says, "hear."

The teacher praises him. "That's better."

"Akimoto?"

"Here!"

The roll call continues until most of the students are accounted for. The teacher then continues.

"Kenta?"

There's no answer.

"Where's Kenta?"

Ippei, the boy who usually answers such kind of questions, raises his hand. "He was on the bus this morning. He sat in back . . . far in back 'cause he wanted sleep. I think he's still sleeping on the bus." (Everyone laughs again.)

"Hum. Come to think of it, he did look very tired in class yesterday . . . Now, let's see, where were we?" (Pause) "Does anyone remember? Ha, ha! Just joking. Of course: verbs. We were studying verbs. Tricky little things, aren't they?"

Ippei raises his hand. "Should I go see if Kenta is still sleeping on the bus? It's parked in front."

"No, no. If Kenta is that tired, let him sleep. I'm sure he'd prefer that to studying . . . studying . . ." What were we studying? Oh, yes, verbs. (Pause as the teacher looks for someone who looks more awake than others.)

Tomoko, a girl sitting in the front row, looks alert. "Tomoko, can you give us an example of a transitive verb? Not an intransitive one, a transitive verb. I want a transitive verb. Do you understand, Tomoko?"

The student looks up at the teacher, squinching as if the sun were beaming into her eyes. She smiles. Then she pauses (a very long pause). Then she turns to the student sitting on her right, leans over and they begin to mumble something. Then, sitting upright again, once more, she pauses, rubs her chin and, a few seconds later, pulls at a few strands of hair, gazing at them nonchalantly. After a few seconds she turns to the student sitting on the other side. Again, there's a short powwow. Finally, she turns back to face the teacher. Another smile . . . and another squint. Then, after another long pause, she opens her mouth and out it comes: "Pardon?"

The reaction is immediate: the teacher grimaces, opens his hands, and then lifts his arms upwards as if in fervent prayer. But the gesture is only momentary, since Ippei calls him to attention.

"Teacher, you are OK? Not sick?"

Gathering his composure, the teacher miraculously manages a smile. All the students smile, too, whether out of their naturally disposed good heartedness or out of a malicious intent to deceive him into thinking they're sincerely interested in learning English—he's not quite sure. Then suddenly, as if by the loving grace of almighty God, the thought then passes through his mind: patient . . . be patient. Humor them! Whatever happens, humor them!

"Tomoko, what I'm looking for is a verb, you know, like "beat," "strike," "hammer," "tear apart," "crush," "scream"—something like that." (Big pause) "OK, let me give you an example. How about this: 'Tom saw the donkey.' See? '*Saw*.'" (Despite himself, he had a bit of a chuckle at that one.) "That's a transitive verb. Transitive. It's a verb that takes a direct object . . . direct. OK, got that? (He pronounces the words very slowly and distinctly.) Do . . . you . . . understand?" (Pause) "Now, let's try again. Who can give me an example of a transitive verb, I mean, in a sentence? Give me an example of a transitive verb in a sentence, an English sentence, not a Japanese sentence."

The students all start talking to one another. Little by little, the commotion settles down, then glides to a complete silence. The eyes are all down now, glued either to the floor, to their desks or, in Tomoko's case, to the strands of her bleached hair. However, one, Kayo, is gazing out the window. Maybe that means something.

"Kayo, how about you? Can you give us an example of a transitive verb?"

Kayo pauses, then smiles confidently. "Yes, I can. 'The donkey saw Tom.'"

The whole class begins to laugh, even the teacher. "Ha! Ha! That's good, Kayo! That's very good! 'The donkey saw Tom.' Ha! Kayo, I can see you're heading for a bright future. Maybe someday you, too, will be lucky enough to teach Freshman English. Wouldn't you love that?" Nobody responds. (Is it that bad?)

The teacher now begins to page quickly through his notes. "Hum, let's see, where are we? Where are we? Oh, yes, yes, of course: the speeches . . . the next thing are the speeches. OK, who is our first speaker? Reiko, do you know? Do you know who our first speaker is, our first one?" (Over the years he'd somehow gotten into the habit of repeating things over and over.)

"Yes, teacher."

"Good. Good for you, Reiko. Now, are you ready? Are . . . you . . . ready, Reiko?"

"Yes, I am ready, teacher."

"Fine. . . fine. Please come up here, up here, and write your name on the board. Write here on the board. (He points to a spot on the board.) And, oh, I almost forgot: here are some papers. Everyone take a sheet . . . take one sheet of paper, just one, not two, just one. Good. Now, while Reiko is speaking, or after she finishes, write down your remarks. Write your (he stresses each syllable) re-flec-tions. So while, during, or after Reiko's speech, write. Do you understand? Does everyone understand? Did she speak loudly? Did she use gestures? You know, ges-tures?" He opens his arms, raises them high, and opens them out again. "How was her pro-nun-ci-a-tion? Did she have good eye contact, I mean, did she look directly at us? All right. Here we go. Now, Reiko, please . . ." He motions for the student to come up to the front, while he takes a seat at the back of the room. Everyone's attention rivets on the student standing before the teacher's desk.

The student takes a low bow, clears her throat, and begins.

"Hello, everyone!"

All the students greet her with their own "Hello!"

"Today I'd like to talk with my cat."

The teacher quickly raises his hand in a "WAIT!" signal. He then scribbles something quickly in big letters on a piece of paper and holds it up high. The communication succeeds.

"Today I'd like to talk about my cat."

  "I have a cat. His name is 'Michael.'" (Some laughter.) "My cat is masculine. When my cat is born, mother called him 'Yuki' [Snow], because he was born in winter. But I said, 'No, he shall be called 'Michael.'" 'Why?' said mother. 'Because it is Professor Michael's name,' I said." (More laughter.)

"I am going to speak a story. It is truth."

"Two years before, we had Akiko's birthday party, my little sister. We ate *dango* [dumplings] and cake and other stuff. I was filled up. Everybody was filled up. They went back to home, and we went back to bed. Then my father had Michael on his chest. He was scratching on his face. Father woke. Oh! Oh! He saw smoke. It was fire. "Oh, awake! Awake! Everyone, awake! Quick!" Father saw the curtains with fire and threw it out the windows. It was next to the heater and got fired. Michael saved us. What a good cat! He's my favorite cat. I love him."

"Thank you for your listening."

The students bent their heads and began to scribble feverishly. Total silence. (Heaven on earth!) The teacher also began to jot down a few of his own observations: "Wonderful speech! A few grammar errors, but very well organized. And very good eye contact. But how about a few gestures? For example, when you said, "two," you could put up two fingers, or when you said, "we ate," pretend that you're eating. Anyway, I liked your speech very much. Nice name for a cat, isn't it?"

While a few of the students were still writing their evaluations, the teacher glanced at the clock: 11:45. Fifteen minutes to go. What to do? Then, up at the front again, an idea popped into his head.

"OK, everybody, let's all stand up. Now, we're going to play a little game. Each one has to ask me a question. After you ask the question, you can sit down again. OK?" The students look at one another, wondering how difficult it might be to do such a task. However, after a few seconds, one of the boys in the back raises his hand.

"Teacher, how old are you?"

"Oh, I forgot. You can ask any question, except for that one. Try again, Jun."

A different student, Kyoko, raises her hand.

"Are you married?"

"No."

The ball begins to roll, as the hands go up.

"How many children do you have?"

The teacher just smiles, as several of the students pooh-pooh her question. The student remains standing.

"Do you like Japan?"

"Yes, very much."

"Do you like sushi?"

"Yes, I do."

"What's you favorite place in Japan?"

"Kyoto."

"Do you like to dance?" (Everyone laughs.)

"Yes, but I haven't danced in a long time."

"Did you ever have a girl friend?"

(Hum . . . how to answer that one?)

"Yes." (Everyone seems to perk up even more.)

Only a few students were still standing. And, for some reason or other, as the questions seemed to be focusing more and more on something he only had a dim intuition about, he felt himself becoming a bit tense.

"Do you ever get homesick?"

(Another hum . . .)

"Yes, a little."

"Are you happy?" (This came from Ippei, who until now never said anything so personal.)

"Yes, I think so."

"Will you live in Japan forever?"

"Yes, I would like to."

"Why did you come to Japan?"

"To teach you."

(A long pause)

"Do you like this class?"

The teacher paused. He never thought they would ask such questions. But now, for the first time ever, he knew that it was much more than grammar that they were after. They wanted contact. And they wanted someone who cared about them, even if they made all kinds of stupid mistakes. They wanted more. And now it was becoming clearer—much clearer. Now he knew. Now he knew.

"Oh, ah, sorry, I, I was thinking about something else. Yes, yes, of course. Of course, I like this class. Why not?"

It was true: something was definitely beginning to tighten in his throat, so much so that he began to think of how he could bring things to a close. Then suddenly, an idea popped into his head.

"OK, everybody. There's a football game tomorrow, and Norio is playing. I guess that's a good enough excuse. So, lucky you: no homework. Get a good rest. And see you on Monday, ten-thirty sharp. If Kenta is sleeping, carry him here. It's better than sleeping in a bus. Maybe he can learn something by osmosis. Osmo-sis! Look it up in the dictionary!"

THE TOUR GUIDE

"Hello! Can I help you?"

"Oh, yes, yes, thanks!"

"All right. Please take a seat. Good. Let's see. Can you please give me your name?"

"White, Michael."

"Thank you, Mr. White! Now, what can I do for you?"

"Well, actually, I'm a . . . a bit desperate. Take anything you've got. Anything, doesn't matter."

"I see. Well, that should be easy. OK, just a few questions first, just to fill me in a bit. Can you tell me what kind of work you've been doing till now, what kind of experience?"

"Sure." (He pushes a paper across the desk.) "Here's my resume. Pretty short, but . . ."

The manager begins to read it. "Hum, quite a background. But, what's this? Are you a priest?"

"Yes."

"And what's this about Japan? Do you live in Japan?"

"Yes, I teach there. English and religion."

"Oh, I see. But what are you doing here?"

"Well, it's a long story, a bit complicated. I've been in Japan for six years, always teaching, except for studying Japanese in the beginning."

"I see. But how come you're here? I mean, I'd expect you to be at a church somewhere. Are you still a priest?"

"Yes, I'm still a priest. But, you see, ever since ages ago, it's been one school after another. After ordination, graduate school, then Japan and Japanese. After that, teaching. So, that's it. That's why I asked for a sabbatical. It came through, so here I am."

"But why an employment agency? Why not a church?"

"It's for a change—get some experience working. After that, it's back to Japan and, hopefully, having learned a lot about how people earn their daily bread."

"I see. That explains it: you want some practical experience. OK, now, have you done anything since you came back from Japan, any kind of job?"

"Yes. Actually, a variety of things."

"Such as?"

"Well, the first job I had was at a pet shop, taking care of the animals—feeding them, cleaning up . . . that kind of thing. But, well, that didn't work out so well."

"Oh! Why not?"

"Well, to tell the truth, I liked it, I mean being with the animals and birds and things. Nice atmosphere . . . different sounds—like a little jungle with everybody pitching in. But, well, unfortunately, it didn't last long, just a few weeks, actually. You see, well, it was a kind of small place and we weren't making much money. Cuckoos weren't selling so well in those days. So one day, I got this bright idea to increase the bird-count, which, of course, would mean more income. Good idea, right? Wrong! I mean, well, one day I mixed in some Viagra with the bird-feed. (Didn't tell the boss, of course.) And it worked. I mean, you should have seen the place. They were laying eggs by the dozens, I mean, just popping them like . . . like popcorn. But the trouble was, we didn't have enough bird cages. Even worse, they weren't singing anymore. All they could think about was, well, you know, making more babies. But, oh, God! When the boss found out what was going on, he took me to the back room and said two unforgettable words."

"Oh! What did he say"?

"*You're fired*!"

(The manager begins to laugh, then holds it in.) "I see. Gee, that's too bad—very unfortunate. Well, how about after that? Did you get a job after that?"

"That was worse."

"Worse? Why's that?"

"Well, you see, liking animals, I got this job at the zoo—you know, at Nay Aug Park. It was easy, just the night shift, checking to see if the doors were locked, lights out—that kind of thing. Oh, and making sure that the animals had enough water. Well, around two in the morning, I was sleepy as hell and wasn't paying much attention. All the monkeys were dozing at the back of their cage, and all I had to do was to fill their water-tank by turning on the faucet inside the cage. But after I did that, I forgot to lock the door. Next morning, I was having breakfast at home and—you wouldn't believe it! There was this news, right on TV, showing a bunch of monkeys on top of the zoo throwing their shit down at the kids below."

(Again, the clerk suppresses a laugh.) "Oh, my! Sounds awful. What happened then?"

"Oh, God, you should have heard him. He was furious— the boss, I mean. 'Pack up!' he said, 'and don't come back! Or I'll put *you* in the monkey cage! Throwing shit at the children! God almighty!' And that was the end of that."

"Hum! That was tough luck, too, wasn't it? So, well, OK. I guess that's enough about the past. Now, let's see. (He shuffles through some papers on his desk.) Oh, good, a few offers! Let's see . . . Hum. Ever do any construction work: carpentry, plumbing, masonry— that kind of thing?"

"No, sorry!"

"I see. How 'about teaching? Oh, I forgot; you want to take a break from that."

" Yes. Yes, we can let that one slide."

"OK, as you say." (He searches through some more pages.) "Oh, here! Here's something: truck driver. Ever drive a truck before?"

"Oh, no; you can skip that, too. But, well, yes, actually, I did that, too."

"Well?"

"That didn't work out either."

"Why not?"

"Well, after the zoo stuff, I got this job at a construction site. Wasn't hard, I mean, driving. It was a big thing, a concrete mixer. I'd just drive to the place indicated, plug things up, and wait. When the tank was emptied, I was finished. Simple. But, well, as I said, that didn't work out either."

"Why not?"

"Well, one day, the boss told me to take a load over to River Street—745 River Street. Seems like some guy was building something and wanted some cement. Anyway, when I got there, I couldn't find the place. Walked up and down a trillion times. Then I noticed something in the back of one of the houses. It was a small pool and, beside it, a pile of sand—other stuff, too: bricks, wires, boards—things like that. So I figured somebody had decided to get rid of the pool and that they'd made a mistake at the office. It should have been 735 River Street, not 745. Anyway, I drove the truck back there and parked. Then, just to be sure, I checked at the house there, but nobody answered. Well, you know, you can't keep cement rolling around forever, so I just went ahead, put in the nozzle, and pushed the button. Then—God, I'll never forget it! This lady comes walking up the alley. When she saw the truck and the cement filling up the pool—you wouldn't believe it—all hell broke loose and she starts screaming. Worse, she pulls some tomatoes out of her bag and starts throwing them at me. "Idiot, you idiot!" she's yelling. "What're ya doin' to my pool?" Then she tells this wolf besides her, "Sic him, tiger! Sic him!" Well, l tell you, I didn't stick around to say goodbye. I took off like a bat out of hell. Unfortunately, I forgot to press the STOP button and so, there we go flying down River Street with the cement pouring out the back. God! You should have seen it! It took them three months to clean up the mess. I won't tell you what the boss said the next day when I showed up for work."

(Another suppressed laugh.) "I see. Tough luck there, too, wasn't it?" He continues to search through the brochure. "Oh, look! Here's something! A guide. They need a guide up at McDade's. How 'bout that?"

"A guide? No, I don't think so. I have a terrible sense of direction."

"That doesn't matter. You can't get lost in a mine." (Or can you? he muses.) "Oh, here it is." He reads the advertisement: *Wanted: Friendly guide to show visitors the only coal mine park this side of the Mississippi. Very few requirements, just a general understanding of the history of coal mining in northeastern Pennsylvania and some basic points about mining. Prior applicants given preference.*

"How 'bout it? How does that sound?"

"Well, I don't know. I was never good in history. And I don't know a thing about coal mining. But, God, I'm desperate. Eating peanuts for supper every night. OK, OK, sign me up. I'll give it a try."

"That's the spirit. Oh, look! You're in luck. There's an interview next Monday. Oh, I almost forgot. They sent this booklet some time ago—all about the mine. Read it carefully. You'll be an expert on mining, right? I know you'll get the job."

Nine people—five women, two men and two children, aged eight and nine, plus the guide and a conductor—ride a small trolly as they make their way jerkily down a mine shaft. A few voices can be heard in the dark, one being Milly, wife of the retired mayor; the other, Nancy, her friend.

Milly: "Oh, Nancy! I'm so excited! Just think, we're going down to the *bowels* of the earth."

Nancy: "Well, not quite that far, dear. Just a wee bit down, you know."

Milly: "Yes, yes! And just think, we're *reliving* history. That's just what we're doing, we're *reliving* the history of America!"

Nancy: "Well, part of it, anyway."

After a few minutes, the trolly comes to a halt. The passengers disembark and follow the guide through a short passageway until they reach a large, rectangular room. A dimly lit bulb hangs overhead affording just enough light to show a few mannequin figures digging away with a drill at some coal lodged inside a crevice. Michael moves to one side of the figures, takes a deep breath, mutters a quick prayer—"Oh, Lord, please send thy most unworthy servant some . . . some . . . *wisdom*"—and begins his speech.

"Ladies and gentlemen, and . . . and children! Here you see some miners at work. You will notice that they are stooped over, the roof being but a short distance from the floor. It must have been quite strain to work like that for so many hours every day, don't you think so?"

This pricks Milly's attention. "How many hours was it?"

Michael: "Ten . . . eleven, sometimes longer—from five in the morning till five in the afternoon."

Milly, counting on her fingers: "Five in the morning! Why so early?"

Michael: "Well, you see, there were children here, too. And they had to make it to school. If they'd start working at five, they'd have a few hours under their belt."

Milly: "Oh, were there children here?"

Michael: "Oh, yes, many."

Milly: "What did they do?"

Michael: "They helped the miners. And, oh, yes, when the coal was extracted, it was put on belts and went upstairs."

Milly: "Upstairs?"

Michael: "Yes, I mean, outside . . . It went outside. The children were there, too."

Milly: "What did they do there?

Michael: "That's where they separated the rocks and slate from the coal." (Pause. No more questions, thank God.) "OK, folks, just follow me! And keep your heads down, please! It's a low passage."

After a short walk, they come to another large room. The figure of a man stands beside a small cart straddling some rails. And hooked to the cart is a donkey.

Milly notices a cage hanging from a corner in the room. "What's that?" she asks, pointing to the cage.

Michael: "Oh, that's a cage . . . for the canaries. They kept canaries with them while they worked."

Jim, one of the tourists, raises his hand and asks, "Why's that?"

Michael: Well, you see, that is . . . ah . . ." (He tries desperately to remember something about the canaries . . .). "It's for observation. That's why the canary is there, for observation."

Jim: "Observation? What does he observe?"

Michael: "The donkey."

Jim: "The donkey!"

Michael: "That's right! You see that donkey? Well, now and then, as is true for all animals, sometimes he had to . . . ah, do his duty. That's what he had to do, his duty. And that's why the canary is there: for observation."

Jim: "Sorry, I don't get it."

Michael: "Well, you see, it's a warning. When the miners heard the canary, they knew some stuff was around. That's what the canary was telling them. Be careful! Don't step on it! (Pause) And that's why they had the canary."

Milly: "Amazing!"

Jim (He doesn't give up.): "But wait! How can anyone see it? It's dark down here! How can anyone see it?"

Michael: "Right! That's why they have those lights on their helmets—to see it."

Jim scratches his head and looks at another man, who hunches his shoulders.

Michael (in a big hurry to change the topic) continues: "OK, folks, let's make a little turn here and move in a bit further."

After passing through a narrow tunnel, they come to another room. Two tall figures stand watching two smaller ones about to shovel some coal into a small wagon. The tour guide motions everyone to draw closer; then he begins his explanation.

"Looks like hard work, doesn't it? And look at the faces of the boys! Black as coal." (An idea suddenly enters his mind.) "I wonder, can anyone tell us why their faces are so dark?"

A tall man, Paul, quickly offers an explanation. "It's the coal and the dust. All that dust makes them black like that."

Michael is quick to add a few remarks. "Well, yes, that's true, that's true. But, well, there's something else, you know. You see, those boys aren't what you think they are. No, sir, not what you think. They're not white; they're black—black slaves, er, runaway slaves."

Everyone stands in silent awe.

"Yes, that's right. They're genuine black slaves. Hands, feet, legs . . . genuine slaves, er, ex-slaves."

Jim's face puckers into a frown. "Hey, wait a minute! That's impossible! There's weren't any slaves in Pennsylvania. Not at that time."

Sensing a chance to take the lead again, Michael decides to let it flow.

"Well, folks, it's a long story, but . . . Well, as I'm sure you know, those fellows had a tough time, I mean, especially down there in New Orleans. And so, one night they made a decision. 'We gotta git otter here! Dis place ain't for us!' And so they did. Moving northwards, they crossed into Texas. But it wasn't a good decision because they ran into trouble with a tribe of Aztecs. Those guys were really fierce. So, once again, they made a break for it. Up they went to the Oregon Trail. That was better, except for the buffalo. There were thousands of them all over the place. But anyway, at least they had plenty of filet mignon to eat. But after a while, they felt enough is enough, so they decided to move on. When they reached Utah, the Mormons tried to convert them, but that didn't work out because, you know, Negro spirituals don't mix with "Awake, Ye Saints of God, Awake!" so that was that. Then they crossed over to Missouri, swam the Mississippi, and made it into Colorado. But—one difficulty after another—it snowed. 'We gotta git otter here, too,' they said, 'afore we freeze to death!' And so they continued their journey eastward into Georgia. That was better, of course, because the Indians let them stay in their wigwams. Well, the rest is history. When they made it to Washington, they met Lincoln, and he welcomed them. 'I have a dream,' he said, 'that all men are created equal.' Well, you should have seen them jump for joy when they heard that. And so they continued their journey into Pennsylvania. That's when Wilhelm Penn told them they could stay there forever because he needed people to fill up his woods. But, you see, they were afraid because a lot of people wanted to catch them and send them back to New Orleans. But they said, 'No way!' And what did they do? They decided to work in the mines. In that way, nobody could know that there were any slaves in Pennsylvania. So there we are."

Millie, almost in tears blurts out, "Oh, those poor dears!"

Michael, deciding the moment was right for a quick exit, directs the group toward the trolly. After boarding, they sit in silence. (Overwhelmed by Michael's final speech? Meditative about what they're seen and heard in the mine? Hard to tell.) Having reaching the entrance to the tunnel, they disembark, most of them heading for the gift shop, except for the two children and their parents, who make their way to the main office. "Oh, Oh!" he thought. "They're going to spill the beans—tell the chief all the bullarkey about the way the miners worked. Oh, well, it was fine while it lasted. Might as well turn in the uniform. Good as a gonner now . . ."

As he made his way to the office, he saw the family moving toward the parking lot. Surprisingly, before they got into their car, all four of them gave him a big wave. What's that? Were they smiling? Oh, well, at least they had the decency to wave good-bye.

The bell jingled as he entered. Hearing it, the manager jumped up from his desk. "Michael, please, have a seat, have a seat! Coffee? Tea? Some cake? Listen, I never heard anyone praise a guide like that family praised you. Honest to God! I mean, when you first came here, I was wondering, I mean, seeing your job record and all that. But you should have heard those people talk about the tour! And the canary! That was brilliant! The kids were fascinated . . . said they'd tell everybody at school.

Michael, listen! I'm giving you a promotion. You're on full time now. And you're in charge of all the guides. They need somebody like you, I mean, you know, somebody with a bit of . . . of . . . *imagination*. Listen! From now on, I want you to talk to all the guides every Monday morning. Loosen them up . . . add some humor . . . I'm sure you know what I mean."

It was hard to fall asleep that night. But when he did, the dreams came rolling in. A canary was singing somewhere from the branch of a tree and a donkey was heehawing in tune underneath. Children were running around in the grass playing with a soccer ball. A little girl with a long blonde ponytail was throwing a ball to a boy with black skin and curly hair. Others were taking turns having fun riding up and down an escalator. And over on the side was a group of adults sitting at a table and busy filling their plates with pipping hot beef tenderloin. "My, look at all the meat!" said one of the women as she lifted a large slice of filet from the skittle. "Enough to feed a tribe."

The alarm ended the dream, but not the feeling. He felt happy. It was a new day and life would never be the same. He didn't know how, but he knew that from now on, life would never be quite the same.

DRIVING ME CRAZY

"Now, Mr. White, if you would kindly sit here, I'll adjust the computer." (He adjusts the computer to the beginning of the test.)

"OK, looks fine now. Now, as you know, Mr. White, this is the first step to getting your driver's license. I'm afraid the questions are a bit difficult but, well, with the weather conditions here in Pennsylvania quite severe sometimes, especially in winter, we want to be sure that you are familiar with all the rules. All right, that said, this is how it works. There are eighteen questions. They will appear on the screen one by one. If you agree with the statement given on the screen, just push the YES frame. If you disagree, push the NO frame. You will have one minute to answer each question. Then the computer will automatically advance to the next question and continue until the end of the test. It's simple. Do you have any questions?"

"No, sir, I understand everything all right."

"Good. I will come back when the test is completed. Good luck!"

Just about the time he finished settling into a comfortable position, the first question appeared. "If you were crossing some railroad tracks and you saw a train barreling down on you, you should jump out of the car and run like hell."

Let's see, he thought. Eeny, meeny, miny, mo . . . He tapped the YES frame

Immediately, a pesky little word appeared: WRONG.

Oops! That was a tough one, he thought. Maybe the next one is easier.

The computer raced ahead and, in a few seconds, showed the second question. "If you were driving on a highway and saw a deer standing in the middle of the road, you should roll down the window and yell at him; for example, you should say, "Hey, get off the road, you bugger!"

Hah! he thought. That's just common sense. Again, he pushed the YES sign, and again came the answer: WRONG.

Oh, my goodness, he thought, these questions aren't so easy. But, no doubt about it, they always put the hard questions at the beginning. Should be easier from now on.

In a few seconds, the third question appeared. "You are approaching an intersection and see a yellow light flashing. You should step on the gas pedal and rush ahead before the light turns red."

Ah! he thought again, everybody does that. He pushed the YES frame, after which—mercilessly— the answer read, again: WRONG. "Ohhhh . . . !"

At this point, he made a quick calculation. Hum: three wrong. That means I have to get all the other questions right. OK, Michael, thinking cap . . . put on the thinking cap! And slow down, slow down! That's the problem: You're moving too quickly. Not enough thought. OK, ready now. Little Flower, show your power!

Whether by sheer luck, or from past experience—it certainly wasn't because he had studied the driving manual—he happened to get the next question right. And when the "CORRECT" sign appeared, he let out a yell, which reaction drew the attention of a long line of people waiting to apply for the next test, but also a frown from a policeman at the front desk. No matter: he was on the winning track now and nothing could hold him back. Down, down, down with the devil!

Recollecting an examination he had taken years ago, a light flashed through his mind. Let's see! The first three questions were all negative; then came a YES. I bet the next two are also YES. In a few seconds, another question crossed the screen. "You are about to come to an intersection. After arriving there, you intend to turn to another road on your right side. There are no cars in sight behind your vehicle. Is it still necessary to use your turn signal before arriving at the intersection?"

Haven't the slightest idea, he thought, but, what the heck, let's give it a YES.

Immediately, the screen flashed: CORRECT.

Sixth question: "Your friend at a party offers you a martini before you drive home. Despite all the pressure, you hold up your hand as a sign of refusal and say, 'No, sir (or madam, as the case may be)! I must obey the driving rules of the State of Pennsylvania!' You made a wise decision."

Another YES, another CORRECT, sure as sure can be!

Ah, isn't that interesting! Three NO's and three YES's. So that's the pattern!

Seventh question: "You are driving along and want to check if your horn is working properly. Press down hard on the horn and listen to the sound."

"NO."

A welcome "CORRECT" answer smiles across the screen.

Now that he knew the pattern — three NO's, followed by three YES's — he didn't bother to read the questions anymore when they came up on the screen. Delightedly, he watched the CORRECT signal pop up all the way to the end of the test. At that point, the good news crossed the screen: PASSED.

In a few seconds, the same officer who had given him the initial instructions approached. "Congratulations, Mr. White! Looks like you studied the manual quite well."

"Thank you, sir, thank you! Well, I admit it was pretty tough, but, well, it all depends on one's attitude. That's the secret: a positive attitude! It works every time!"

"You don't say!" (Pause, as the officer scribbles something on a piece of paper.) All right; now, if you'll just take this slip and step outside there. The driving course is a bit tricky, but I don't think you'll have any trouble, not with your, ah, attitude."

"Thanks, again, sir. I'll do my best."

Outside, he waited a while. Presently, a policeman signaled for him to approach closer and to step into a waiting car. Having done so, he buckled the seat belt and waited. After a few seconds, another policeman stepped into the car. He was a big man and quite heavy and so, to give himself more leg room, he pushed his seat as far back as it would go. Before starting out, he went through the regular formulas, first, with the name.

"Let's see, 'White,' is it? 'Mr. Michael White'"?

"Yes, sir, that's correct."

"All right, now, Mr. White. I'm sure you're aware of the laws of Pennsylvania. Here's the first: *When driving an automobile, the said driver must not infringe on any of the state laws. Regulations stipulate exactly what the driver must do in order to remain a law-abiding, peace-loving citizen.* Now, Mr. White, tell me, do you understand what I'm saying? Is everything clear?"

"Yes, sir, clear, very clear, sir."

"Good! Now, pull out from here, and let's being the test."

(The car moves slowly through the Driving Center out towards a two-lane highway.)

"Now, as I was saying, Mr. White, it is of the utmost importance that you obey every road mark, every direction signal, and all pertinent signs—every one. Any deviation from the stipulated rules will merit an immediate curtail. Therefore . . . WAAAH! . . . OOOOH! . . . YAAAH! . . . MOVE! MOVE OVER! LEFT! LEEEFT! Jesus, that was close! Didn't you see that old lady pushing the buggy back there? God, we almost ran over her!"

"Oh, so sorry, sir! Sorry! It won't happen again, sir, I assure you. Never again. Never, ever!"

"Well, I hope not, I certainly hope not. Whew, that was a close one. Thought I'd be attending a funeral tonight. OK, now just go ahead—slooowly. And, please, Mr. White, watch out for pedestrians on the side of the road, OK?"

"Yes, sir, I will, sir, watch for all pedestrians, watch all the time. I'll keep my eyes open, sir, watching all the time!"

"Good! That's good. So, let's see, where were we? Oh, yes, the laws. Ah, here it is: *Thus, the driver of the said vehicle must take due caution in order to remain a law-abiding, peace-loving citizen. Therefore, any infringement of the rules, no matter now minor, will automatically result in an immediate suspension of the said license.*' Do you understand, Mr. White? Let me hear it from your own mouth: DO YOU UNDERSTAND?"

"Yes, sir. Understand. I understand everything. Everything, just as you said, er, read, sir."

"Good! That's good! I'm glad we're clear about that. And now for point ninety-eight: *So if any of the set rules are either overlooked, ignored, or the object of downright contempt, the said driver shall be shorn of his license, subjected, moreover* . . . WAAAH! . . . OOOH! . . . OOOH! . . . NOOO! . . . WAAAH! . . . WATCH OUT! . . . TRUCK! . . . RIGHT! . . . GO RIGHT! . . . RIIIIIGHT! Oh, my God! (He wipes some perspiration from his forehead.) That was close! Jesus! Mr. White, don't you know? You're supposed to drive in the *center* of the lane. Do you get it? The *center*! Not on the right side of the road. Not on the left. In the CENTER! Jesus, that was close. You almost swiped that big truck back there. Do you realize that? Please, PLEASE, Mr. White. Obey the rules, OK? Drive in the *center* of the lane. The CENTER!"

"Yes, sir, I've got it now: the center. Not to worry. That's just what I'll do. Right in the center of the road. Just as you say, sir, right up the middle!"

"Well, I certainly hope so. Jeez! (He wipes his face again.) "So, now for the last part of the guidebook . . . *And if the driver should make any kind of objection to the predetermined rules, his license must be revoked immediately. In fact, in certain circumstances, such a driver may be liable to immediate prosecution, at which time THE BOOK WILL BE THROWN AT HIM AND THE RECKLESS WRETCH WILL PAY FOR HIS CRIMINAL ACTIVITIES BEHIND PRISON BARS.* Well, Mr. White, I realize that these are harsh words, very harsh, and you can be sure that I didn't write them.

But you wouldn't believe the kind of people who come here to get their license. Honestly! Why just the other day, I . . . OOOH! . . . WAAAH . . . OOOH! . . . JESUS, MARY, JOOOSEPH!"

(After the car passes through a busy intersection, the dialogue continues.)

"Sir, sir! Are you . . . are you all right? Sir, why are you sitting on the floor like that? Heart attack? Fever? Stroke? Sir, sir, can you hear me? Over and out . . . CAN . . . YOU . . . HEAR . . . ME, SIR?"

(The officer manages to rise slowly from the floor and take his seat again.)

"Jus' . . . jus' don't say anything . . . don't say anything! Jus' . . . jus' . . . pull over . . . pull over here!"

The car pulls over slowly to the side of the road, and the policeman and driver exchange places. The officer, close to the point of having a nervous breakdown, drives back to the Center, his eyes fixed straight ahead as if he'd just been hit by a bolt of lightning. He pulls the car into the Center and parks, still staring ahead. After a few minutes, he seems to calm down a little.

"Mr. White, please . . . allow . . . allow me to ask you a few questions. First, where do you live? It says something here on your application about Japan. Do you live in Japan?"

"Yes, sir, that's where I live. Nice country it is, very nice country. Friendly people, you know—always smiling, very polite and . . ."

"Yes, yes, I'm sure it, er, they are. But if you live in Japan, why are you applying for a Pennsylvania license?"

"Well, you see, sir, I come home once every few years. And I figure that if I had a Pennsylvania license, I wouldn't have to get an international license every time. That's a good idea. Don't you think so?"

"Huh? Oh, yes, yes, good idea, good idea. (Pause) "And, un, Mr. White, when do you plan on returning to Japan, if I may ask?"

"Tomorrow."

"Tomorrow! You mean you're actually leaving tomorrow for Japan?"

"That's right, sir."

"And when do you plan to come back to Pennsylvania again?"

"Oh, that would be three years from now, three years."

(The policeman scratches his head pensively.) "Hum . . . is that so? And when you come back to Pennsylvania next time, how long do you plan on staying?"

"Oh, I don't know. Maybe three or four weeks."

"Only three or four weeks?"

"So, tell me, sir, tell me straight. How'd I do? I mean, did I pass? Can I get my driver's license? You can tell me straight, sir. I can take the news, good or bad. No problem. Then I can inform my uncle."

"Pardon?"

"Yes, then I can inform my uncle, Larry. He's the one who told me to get the license here."

"Your uncle Larry. You mean, Larry White?"

"Yes, sir. As you know, he's in charge of the office in the Hiring and Firing Department in Harrisburg. I'm sure you know the Hiring and Firing Department, sir. And I'm sure he'll be thrilled when he hears the good news. Of course, sir, I wouldn't want anything like that to influence your decision, not at all. Of course, my uncle, who is in charge of the Hiring and Firing Department, would be thrilled to hear that I passed, don't you think so, sir? He'd really be thrilled."

"The policeman mumbles in a low voice: "Yeah, thrilled, I'm sure." Then he takes his pen and scribbles something on a form.

"All right, Mr. White, you win, er, that is, you passed. Sign here on the dotted line, please. And, ah, if you every have any trouble, I mean, well, that is, if you should ever happen to have a, let's say, a sort of, well, minor mishap—nothing serious, of course—and someone asks you who gave you your license, you just tell them that you got it at the Driving Center. No names mentioned. OK?"

"OK, sir. Thank you, thank you very much! And, yes, I'll do just that. That's just what I'll do. No names mentioned."

"Good! Well, so long, Mr. White. And watch out for the little old ladies, the big trucks, and all the stop signs. And don't forget: the *center* of the road. OK?"

"Sure, sir! You know me—I'll watch out. No problem. No problem at all. Well, sir, I guess that's it. Bye, now. Have a nice day!"

"Thanks, you, too!"

THE CHAIRMAN

"Hello, father? Father Michael, is that you?"

"Yes, I'm Father Michael."

"Good. How are you, father? This is Yuko . . . Yuko Kato."

"Oh, hello, Yuko! How is everything?"

"Fine, fine! A little busy now and then, but I'm OK. Fine. Listen, father, I have a request."

"A request? What kind of request?"

"Well, I know it's rather sudden, but, um, well, we . . . we would like you to be our *rijichoo*."

"*Rijichoo*? Just a second please!" (He quickly reaches over to his Japanese dictionary, flips the pages to the "r" section and, luckily, finds it listed on top of the page: "a director," "a trustee," "a chairman of the board of directors.") At that, he lets out a yelp: "Eh!"

"Pardon?"

"Oh, nothing, sorry! Just a burp—last night's supper. Heh, heh!"

"I'm sorry, father, I know it's all of a sudden, but . . . Listen, are you free tomorrow, Saturday? I have a friend, Ayumi Sato. If you have time, we can meet you and tell you everything. Are you still living on the campus at the Christianity Center? We can meet you there."

"Yes, that's OK. How about ten o'clock?"

"Good. Thank you, father. See you tomorrow."

The next day, at ten o'clock sharp, two middle-aged women enter the Center. Father Michael is waiting for them at a table near the entrance. When they enter, Ms. Kato introduces her friend, Ms. Sato. After a few preliminary remarks, they begin to zero in on the main topic, starting with Ms. Kato's explanation of their plan.

"Father, it's like this. It's a Food Bank. I'm sure you know about Food Banks. If some company is making, ah, let's say, jelly, the company puts a date on the label, which means they have to sell it by a certain day. But if they can't sell everything by then, they just throw it away. That's where we come in. We let food companies know about our work. Then, if they have a lot of food near the cut-off date and can't sell it, instead of throwing it away, they give us a call. If we can use it—and we can use just about everything—they deliver it to us. After that, we give the food to whoever needs it. Very simple. Oh, I forgot to mention that we've been doing this for about a year. But it's time now to make it an organization. Besides, to make things even better, a few weeks ago the bishop said he'd let us use an old building that was formerly a kindergarten. He even said we could use it for free. So, that's it. We've got everything. All we need is a chairman. Father . . . please!"

"I, ah, well, it's very kind of you to make such an offer but, to tell the truth, I've never done anything like that before. Teaching, yes. I'm OK with Shakespeare and Milton and that kind of thing, but I don't have a clue about social work . . . like a babe lost in the woods. I'm sorry, but I'm afraid it's way over my head."

"But, father! You're a priest, right?"

"Yes, that's right."

" And you have a degree, right? What is it, English literature?"

"Yes, that's right!"

"And you're the dean of the English Department at the university, right?"

"Oh, no, no; nothing like that. I'm just an ordinary teacher."

"But you've written some books, right"?

"A few, yes."

"Seven?"

"I forget."

"Oh, father, you're so humble. You're just the person we need, someone we can con . . . er, that is, someone with whom we can cooperate. That's it, co-op-er-ate." (She emphasizes each syllable slowly.) So that's it! You've got status. And that's just what we need—just what we need to get started." (Pause. She doesn't give up.) "Listen, father, there's not much work. We'll make all the connections. All we need is a director, a . . . a name—that's it, a name up front. You know what I mean?"

"That's right," adds Ms. Sato. "We'll do all the work. All we need is a chairman."

"But, what do I do? What would be my responsibilities?"

"Oh, don't worry, father, it's easy. Do you have business cards?"

"Yes."

"OK. How 'bout a stamp, you know, a stamp with your name on it?"

"Yes, I have one."

"Oh, that's wonderful! So, well, you know the Japanese custom. When you meet somebody new, you just give him your card. And if it's something official, like, ah, OK. Let's say you want to buy a car. When you buy it, you put a stamp on the paper. Then it's official. It's your car. I'm sure you know about all that."

"Yes, but about this chairman job. Is that all I have to do, I mean, just hand out my calling cards and stamp things?"

"That's about it, father. It's very simple. As Ayumi said, we'll do all the work. You don't do anything, well, not much anyway. So please don't worry about anything!"

"I see. Well, I . . . I . . . Don't get me wrong. I mean, I appreciate your offer. So I . . . I . . . "As he scratches his chin, Yuko slowly pulls out a sheet of paper from her briefcase. "And, just think, father, you'll have a nice office. And we'll put your name plate on the desk: Father Michael White, Chairman, Food Bank, Nagoya. Isn't that wonderful?"

"Yes, I'm sure it is . . . "

"So, father, all you have to do is sign your name here." She pushes a paper towards him ever so discreetly and, afterwards, reaches across the table to hand him a pen. (She's very well prepared.) He glances up at the ceiling as if to mutter a prayer—"O God, come to my assistance; oh, Lord, make haste to help me!"—takes the pen and writes his name. The women are all smiles.

"Oh, father," she says, "I'm so happy! I can't wait to tell everybody! They'll be thrilled. Thank you, thank you ever so much!"

A long pause ensues, after which Yuko speaks again.

"Oh, father, I forgot to tell you. There's one more thing . . . just a tiny detail, but, well, you see, you're going to be on television."

"Eh! Television! Me? What television?"

"NHK—Japan national television."

"Japan national television!"

"Yes, isn't that wonderful!"

"But, what am I supposed to say? I mean, I've never been on television before—not even on the radio!"

"Oh, you just explain what Food Bank is."

"Explain what Food Bank is! I don't know a thing about Food Bank!"

"Oh, not to worry, father. We'll tell you everything beforehand!"

"Beforehand! Oh, my God! When it is? I mean, when am I supposed to be on TV?"

"Saturday."

"Saturday! You mean this coming Saturday?"

"That's right, father."

"But that's only five days away."

"Yes, but don't worry, you'll have a script. All you have to do is read the script."

"All I have to do is read the script! Wait! Is that in Japanese?"

"Yes, of course! That's the language of the people here."

"You don't say!" (Pause) "And how long am I supposed to speak on television?"

"Oh, not so long. Ten or fifteen minutes. Something like that."

"Ten or fifteen minutes! On NHK, the one that goes all over Japan?"

"No, father, just all over the central part of Japan: Nagoya, Gifu, Mie, Shizuoka ... Some foreign stations also pick it up. Isn't it wonderful, father! You'll be famous."

(Groan) "Yes, I'm sure I will be. Maybe they'll put up a statue someday."

The studio wasn't all that large, just enough for a desk in the front of the room and space for the cameramen to move around here and there. Oh, yes, there were the lights, too, lots of them, mostly in the area behind the cameramen, but a few on the sides of the room and several above and behind the desk. Fortunately, it was a large desk, enough to hide his trembling knees. There was no problem with his hands. Except when turning the pages of the script, he could also hide them beneath the desk.

The minutes ticked away ever so slowly and he could hear the clock tick, tick, ticking away, one nervous tick at a time. Now he knew how people feel when they are about to be shot. He never thought he'd live to see the day.

At precisely 7:45 a.m., the announcer makes his pitch.

Mina san, ohayoo de gozaimasu! Ohayoo, Nippon— Irasshaimase! ("Hello, everyone! Thank you for joining us and welcome to our program, 'Good morning,

Japan!'''"). Once again, we would like to give you the news of the day. But before we do so, I would like to introduce our special guest for today, Father Michael White. We have been informed that Father White is an expert in Food Bank management and distribution. And he would like to tell us how his organization is providing food for thousands of people in our area of Central Japan. Now, without further ado, I would like to turn our attention to Father White. I'm sure he has a great deal to say about his new organization. Father White . . ."

"Thank you, Mr. Ando, for your remarkable introduction. Actually, I'm not such an expert in Food Bank distribution. And to tell the truth, I was a stranger and they took me . . . that is to say, I was persuaded to become the Chairman and Chief Executive Officer of this wonderful organization by some close friends. May the Lord repay them in due course for all they have done."

"Yes," adds the announcer, "I'm sure that your friends deserve a lot of credit for having chosen such a good and experienced leader as you. Now, if you don't mind, I'd like to ask you a few questions about your organization. First of all, can you tell us how you get your food? Where does it come from?"

Father White, sensing the friendliness of the announcer, and suddenly deciding that he knows enough about the organization to answer the questions without relying on the script, pushes it aside. He looks directly at the announcer and says, in as confident a tone of voice as he can muster, "Well, some food companies informed us that they are willing to provide us with their products should there be a surplus."

"Is that so? How many companies promised to help you?"

"Two."

"Two! Only two?"

"Yes, only two. But, of course, we plan on expanding our operations in the near future. Open up. That's the way. By-and-by, we expect more and more companies to fall in line, once they hear about the way our work is progressing."

"Is that so? And how do you plan on expanding?"

"Well, actually, it's a new idea. The original plan was for food companies to tell us if they had a lot of food. If we agreed to accept it, the company would then deliver it to us. The next step would be for us to hand it over to people in need. But, I've come up with a new plan."

"Oh! What's that?"

"Well, once we hear from the company, we'll inform the homeless. Then they can go directly to the company and receive the goods personally. In that way, the company saves gasoline—they don't have to drive from their warehouses to our office to deliver the goods. And, besides, just think of the friendships that will evolve when the homeless get a chance to meet the company staff!"

"I see. But do you think the homeless will do that? I mean, will they go directly to the companies to get the food?"

"Mr. Ando, let me tell you. When a person is hungry, there is no limit to what they will do to get food."

"I see. So your organization will be like, ah, like an intermediary. I mean, you'll get information from the companies and then inform the homeless where to go."

"That's right! That's exactly what we're planning."

"I see. By the way, can you tell us how many homeless are in the Nagoya area?"

"Well, the figure varies from time to time. Right now, it's somewhere between ten and a hundred thousand."

"Between ten and a hundred thousand! That's amazing! I never realized there were so many. Why does it change so much, I mean, the numbers?"

"The weather."

"The weather?"

"Yes. You see, in the summer, it's hot in Nagoya, so the homeless go up north to Hokkaido. There's still some snow up there in the mountains at that time, so they can cool off for a while."

"Amazing! And the winter? Where do they go in the winter?"

"They come back to Nagoya where they can find jobs."

"Jobs? What kind of jobs?"

"Shoveling snow!"

"Shoveling snow! But it only snows once or twice in Nagoya!"

"Yes, but then the city doesn't have to use snow plows. And, besides, it gives the homeless something to do."

"I see." (Pause) "Oh, we still have a few minutes left. Is there anything else you'd like to tell our audience, father?"

"Oh, I might add that I have another plan to keep the homeless occupied."

"How do you propose to do that, father?"

"Well, it's quite simple, actually. They'll become tour guides."

"Tour guides?"

"Yes, that's right. You know, those fellows really get around, I mean, it depends on the work. If there's work somewhere, they'll go there; if not, they stay put. But the fact is, they really get around. Why, some of them even go to Poland and Pittsburg."

"Is that so? Amazing!"

"Yes, isn't it! So I figure that with all that experience going here and there, they'd be ideal tour guides."

"But do they have any training for that kind of thing?"

"Well, that's another thing. You see, I plan on setting up a special course for them at the university."

"A special course?"

"Yes! It'll be entitled, "Tour Guide, 101.""

"Gosh, I never heard of a course like that. But who will teach the course?"

"I will."

"You?"

"That's right! Now I don't want to boast, but to tell the truth, I've read a couple of books by world travelers."

"Really! Who might that be?"

"Well, let's see! There was, ah, that there Laurence of Aribia. He was a great traveler. Got to know the Aribians very well. Very nice people."

"Is that so? Anybody else?"

"Oh, sure, lots of people. What's that lady's name? I mean the one starting with 'Agnes,' or something like that?"

"Agnes? I'm sorry, I can't recall . . ."

"Oh, I got it. Agnes Christ. That's it!"

"Agnes Christ? Do you mean Agnes Christie?"

"That's the very one!" (Pause) "Oh, and there's that Graham Greeney. He went all over the place: China, Africa, Stroudsburg . . ."

"Is that so?"

"Yes, so anyway, that's my plan. I'll teach the homeless how to be tour guides, using literature as a basis. I think that'll keep them busy. On workdays, they'll be guiding; on rest days, they'll be reading."

"I must say, Father, you have some unique ideas. I hope it works out OK."

(Pause, as the announcer glances at the clock.)

"Father White, unfortunately, time has expired. But I must say, this has been one of the most interesting interviews we've ever had. Very original, very, ah— how shall I put it?—very inspiring, very unique. I'm sure our viewers feel the same way. Thank you kindly, father, and I hope that we can have you back here again someday to hear more about how your organization, "Food Bank, Nagoya" is progressing. Thank you, again, for everything."

"Thank you, too, Mr. Ando. It's been a pleasure."

IT ONLY HURTS FOR
A LITTLE WHILE

Ah! Pesty little thing! . . . a bit sore. Guess I'll have to check it out.

A few days later, dressed in a smart tie and newly pressed suit—as if being interviewed for a new job and wanting to impress—he presents himself at the counter, hoping that the woman there is in her nineties, hard of hearing, and blind. Instead, he's disconcerted when he sees Miss Japan, dressed in a neat little uniform, smiling friendly-like at him.

"Yes, may I help you?" comes the dainty voice.

"Well, you see," he blurts out, having forgotten what he had been trying to memorize half of the previous night, "you see, I have this sort of difficulty, nothing serious, of course, just, well, you know, just sort of minor, very minor—sort of. Don't worry about it."

"Un huh. What sort of difficulty is it?"

"Well, you see, it's back there, you know, on the downward side. That's where—back there in the back— in the rear . . . somewhere."

The woman looks puzzled. "Back there? Is there something wrong with your back?"

"Well, no, that is, not exactly. It's back there, but it's not my back. It's . . . well, it's a bit to the bottom, too. Back at the bottom of the back, if you know what I mean. What?"

When the woman screws up her lips as if to say, "No, not exactly," the man tries to clarify things. "Listen, I'll give you a hint: it begins with an "h.""

"Ah, I've got it: it's your heart! You're having some heart pains."

"No, no, that's not it. Fairly close but, no, that's not quite it."

The girl tries again. "Is it your head? Is your head the problem"?

"No, not exactly, but, yes, I mean, sometimes, but not now, only sometimes." He pauses, desperately trying to make himself clear. Just then, a wee bit of a woman standing behind him moves a little forward. "It's his hip, deary. That's what it is, his hip. Poor fellow! I'm having the same trouble myself. Quite painful at times, isn't it?" she says, looking up at the man.

"Is that it?" asks the woman. "Is it your hip?"

"No, I'm afraid not," the man replies. Then, deciding it's time to lead the troops into battle, he leans over the counter as far as he can, cusps his hands around his mouth and whispers as quietly as possible. "It's hemorrhoids. That's what it is, hem . . . or . . . rhoids."

The woman almost bursts out laughing, but suddenly catches herself. "Oh, I see." Then, still trying to restrain herself, she quickly scribbles something on a piece of paper and passes it to him. "Just go up to the second floor and show this at the first window on the left. You're Number Four. One of the nurses will tell you what to do."

"Thanks, thanks very much. Will I see the doctor after that?"

"Yes, I think so. I'm sure the doctor will give you a good checkup."

"Does it hurt?"

Suppressing another giggle, the woman manages to maintain a semi-official tone of voice.

"I'm sure there's not much pain. Just relax and try not to worry."

"Right! Not to worry. That's what I'll do. Thanks, thanks a lot."

Having taken the chit, the man turns and makes his way to the elevator. He daren't take the steps in his grave condition. Each step could be the last.

Exiting the elevator, he was surprised to see such a long corridor full of people waiting to see various doctors— so many that it was difficult to find a seat. But, ah, a kind man, perceiving his debilitated condition, moved to the side, allowing him a place on the bench. Presently, a nurse appeared from one of the rooms and called out, "Number Two!" Ah, he was Number Four. He wouldn't have to agonize for long before the undertaker arrived. The minutes passed, one slow second at a time. Then another nurse appeared. "Number Three!" she called. Ah, to be, or not to be, that is the question. Soon afterwards, another nurse called out, "Number Four!" The man stepped forward and approached the nurse, a bit taken back by her massive bulk. "Michael White?" she said in a loud voice. "Are you Michael White?" If attacked by a bear, he thought, hold your ground, but all he could manage was a little peep. "That's me." "All right," said the woman, "what's the problem?

Having lost his voice (and courage), he handed her the chit. "Here; it's there!"

The nurse held the paper close to her nose. "Hum. Hemorrhoids, is it?"

At once, the whole line jumped to attention, some pointing to Michael, others whispering. "Psst. Did you hear that? Hemorrhoids. He's got hemorrhoids!"

"Nooo! . . . hemorrhoids? You're kidding. And at his age!"

"Yes, that's what she said, hemorrhoids! Poor fellow, dressed so nicely, too! Happens to the best, doesn't it?"

The nurse pointed to a door. "OK, Mr. White, you can go in now."

Dead man walking, he mused as he stepped into the office. "Oh, God!" A young doctor (Miss Japan's sister?), greeted him with a smile. "Hello! Please, make yourself at ease," she said in perfect English. Wondering how he could get out of the room as quickly as he got in, he found himself, again, lost for words.

"Let's see. It says here something about the heart. No, that's crossed out. It's hemorrhoids. I see. All right; now, how long has this been bothering you?"

"Not long, this morning."

"This morning? You mean, you just noticed it this morning?"

"That's right. So it's not so bad." I can make my way home OK, he was tempted to say, but it just didn't come out.

"Well," said the doctor, "let's check up, just to be sure. Could you loosen your belt and lie on the bed there? You can lie on your stomach." (Pause) "All right, that's fine, thank you! Now, Mr. White, this is just a customary procedure. I just want to look a bit closer. It'll only take a few seconds. Are you ready?"

"Who me? Ready? Ready for what?"

For some reason or other, Voltaire's words ran through his mind: "O Lord, make my enemies ridiculous!"

"Don't worry!" said the doctor. "It only hurts for a little while."

"Oh, oh, ooooh!" And it was all over.

"Now, Mr. White, that wasn't so bad, was it?"

"You mean, you're finished? All done?"

"Yes, I'm done. But there's still one more procedure. So if you would just move across the hall, the technician will give you further instructions."

"Further instructions?"

"That's right; it'll only take a short time."

"Oh, good," he thought. "Should be easier after this torture."

After making his way out of the office, another nurse approached and indicated that he should follow her. A few seconds later, they entered a room marked "X-ray." Hardly had he taken his seat when the door opened and who should appear but Beverly, the daughter of his next-door neighbor.

"Oh, it's you, Mr. White! How nice to see you!"

"Beverly!" he exclaimed, "I . . . I didn't know that you worked here."

"Yes," she said, "it's my first assignment after I passed the nurses' exam." (Pause) "Well, I guess we can begin. You can change into this gown. Then sit on the table over there." At that, she disappeared into what looked like the backstage of a movie theater and began to twiddle with this and that.

What's she up to? he mused. Turning on the electricity? Oh, God, give me a break! Naked rats stay cancer free.

The technician emerged from the room and adjusted a large overhead lamp. "Ah, now, Mr. White, I'm just going to insert a little liquid before taking the pictures. Just relax, and don't worry about anything." Then, in a much stronger voice than he expected, she suddenly barked: "LIE DOWN!"

He didn't need further instructions.

That done, she boomed again in the same powerful voice, "ROLL OVER!"

"Oh, God!" he thought, "Naked I came into the world, naked I shall go out."

Suddenly, he felt something cold entering his backside. "Oh, wow, wow, oh, wow . . . !" Then, click! And that was it. Finished. Done.

For some reason or other, as he lifted his body ever so slowly from the table, he couldn't face the nurse. In fact, he had all he could do to get into his slippers, stand up, and waddle towards the door. Once in the corridor, another nurse—so many nurses, and they all knew his name—directed him to take a seat. Ten minutes later, he was back in the doctor's office. He was ready. Cut his throat, pass the poison, shoot the bullet! Anything to get out of here (one way or another).

"Well, Mr. White," said the doctor. "You're in pretty good shape for your age." (What did that mean?) "Just carry on as you've been doing. Don't worry about a thing."

As he made his way down the corridor towards the elevator, he happened to pass by the heavyset woman and, a little later, the X-ray technician. Whether out of respect for his feelings or not, both of them smiled but glanced away as he passed by. So, too, did the pretty secretary at the main entrance. It's funny how feelings work but, for some reason or other, he felt a liking for these people. They were just doing their job. That's all. Just doing their job, one day, one patient at a time. And, come to think of it, they were right: it only hurts for a little while.

FEEDING THE FISH

Louie fixes his gaze forward, puts the van in gear, and pulls out from the curb. Four men occupy the van, plus a cat, just as curious as they are about how this venture is going to pan out. All is absolute silence. At the first stop light, two teenage girls cross in front of the van. Seeing the occupants in the front—a tall, thin man with a long neck behind the wheel and a smaller, heavier man also in front, holding the cat, its head and ears barely visible above the dashboard—they giggle and pass by. Paul, the man holding his purring friend, seems flattered by the attention given by the girls, but the tank commander, Louie, determined to get the vehicle into the thick of the battle, grips the wheel with fierce determination. He has a goal and, by God, he's going to get there.

As Louie steers the van along, he keeps mumbling something under his breath. Is he praying? Singing? Having a stroke? No one seems to know but, wait! Yes, there is: the cat! Whether out of sheer affection or out of a desire to placate Louie, the furry creature takes a glance at him, stretches up and gives him a juicy lick on the chin. Louie's reaction is predictable.

"Jesus, Paul! Take that animal away! He's slobbering all over me!"

"It's not a 'he'! It's a 'she'!"

"Whatever!"

Paul reaches over, lifts the cat, and settles it again on his lap. The cat purrs as Paul scratches behind her ears.

The van speeds along and so, too, does the time: nine, ten, eleven, twelve midnight. At around twelve-thirty, the van pulls slowly into an empty lot. The vague outline of a large ship can be seen a hundred yards out in the bay. The smell of salt water permeates the air.

"Well, here we are!" says Louie with the triumphant note as he glides the van to a stop.

"Here?" queries Michael, coming out of a deep sleep. "Where's here?"

"Here's here!" says Louie, with a voice of authority.

"Great! Where's the hotel?"

"Hotel? What do you mean *hotel*? There isn't any hotel."

"No hotel? You mean we're going to sleep in the van?"

"That's right! In the van."

"How are we going to do that? There are four of us," exclaims Michael."

Louie: "Watch and pray."

"Louie, can I have the key to the back?"

"Sure!" When he hands over the key, Michael exists the van and opens the back to find (luckily) a blanket inside. Unfortunately, however, the blanket is spotted with grease and oil. Oh, well, he thinks, better than nothing. Taking the blanket, he rolls it up and, having returned the key, notices a building at the far end of the lot. As he walks towards it, a slight drizzle begins to fall. A small house stands next to the building, with a two-car garage attached. Hesitant, but with little else to chose from, he stealthily makes his way to the far end of the garage. Two cars occupy most of the space, but there is enough room to unravel the blanket and stretch out his legs. Seeing that a window faces the house immediately next to the garage, he knows he has to be very careful lest the occupants of the house notice his presence. Oops, too late! A glance through the window meets a glance coming from a woman inside the house nursing an infant. But she immediately turns aside, perhaps with an offer of agreement in mind: *if you don't tell anyone you saw me nursing my baby, I won't tell anyone about you. I know it's raining outside; you can stay there for the night.* And with that thought, he decides to unroll the blanket, lie down, and try to get some sleep, into which state he falls in a matter of minutes, tired as he is.

Does the mind have its own clock? He's not sure, but at five o'clock sharp, he's awake. All the lights in the house are off but, even so, he makes his way ever so gingerly out of the garage and back to the van, just in time for some coffee and a sweet roll. Paul and Akio look like they hadn't slept a wink, while Louie, super-charged with the idea of fishing, looks fresh as a daisy. Be as it may, when the thermo empties, Louie gives a signal: "Let's roll!" at which command everyone falls in line, as Job once said, "like straw before the wind."

Several minutes later, the van pulls up in front of an old dilapidated shed. Above the front door hangs a sign in barely legible letters: "CHEAP BOATS AND BAIT SALE." A light inside gives evidence that someone is up and about. Louie pushes a small buzzer at the side of the door and presently a middle-aged man, still wearing pajamas, makes his appearance. A dialogue ensues in due time.

Man: "Help you?"

Louis: "We'd like a boat."

Man: "How big?"

Louise: "For four."

Man: Motor or row?"

Louie: "Motor."

Man: "New or old?"

Louise: "New."

Man: "How long?"

Louie: "All day."

Man: "Five hundred."

Louie: "Two."

Man: "Four."

Louie: "Three."

Man: "Three-seventy-five."

Louie: "Gas included?"

Man: "Yes."

Louie: "Three-forty."

Man: "Three-fifty."

Louie: "Bait?"

Man: "Yes."

Louie: "Three-forty-five."

Man: "Just a second!"

The man re-enters the shed and, after a few minutes, exits again fully dressed. Adept as he is, it takes him but a few minutes to hook a boat to a trailer. He throws a few lifejackets into the boat and then signals everyone to enter his truck. Once at the shore, he frees the boat, sliding it deftly down a ramp and into the water. That done, he gives each a hand as they begin to step into the boat.

"Head towards that bridge," he yells, as Louie manages to start the engine. The big ones are over there."

"Really?" Paul yells back. "What kind?"

"All sorts: halibut, mackerel, butterfish, shark . . . Depends on the current."

"Shark? Are there sharks out there?"

"Plenty."

"Ones that bite?"

"All sharks bite."

Paul's complexion turns a bit white, as he looks at Louie. "Louie, listen, I . . . I've got a headache. Really. And, you know, that wasn't much of a breakfast, was it? I'm still hungry. So is Millie. She hasn't had anything. And, you know, she gets kind of antsy when she hasn't eaten. So, you guys . . . you guys just mosey along. I'll see you later."

"Later?"

"Yeah, when you come back."

"Come back? Oh, come on, Paul! Everything's ready. You can't quit now."

"Why not?"

"Oh, for God's sake! Come on! We've come this far. Don't chicken out now."

Paul sighs. But then his mind jumps ahead as he imagines the teachers laughing when they hear about how he'd backed out. He shrugs, checks Millie's leash, and enters the boat.

Seeing everything more or less in order, the man waves good-bye and leaves.

Due to a slight rainfall, the waves seem somewhat higher than normal, but Louie, seeing this merely as another challenge, steers the boat steadily towards the bridge. Michael takes a seat near Louie in the bow, while Paul and Akio settle in the stern. A tail protruding from Paul's coat reveals the whereabouts of Paul's bosom friend.

Some twenty or so minutes later, Louie turns the engine down just enough to make the boat glide slowly ahead. Then, thinking it's as good a place as any, he cuts the engine. Rods and bait are distributed with a few minor instructions.

"Paul, Akio, you seem OK there. Michael and I'll see what going on here at the sides. That OK with you guys?"

"OK," says Paul, looking a bit whiter than before as he ties Millie's leash to the side of the boat and proceeds to adjust his rod and reel. Like the others, he hooks on a small piece of clam, then drops it nonchalantly over the side the boat. Akio follows suit.

In the meantime, Louie and Michael are hard at it. Every few minutes, they give a yell. "Hey, a bite! Hey, something big is down there!" Presently, Louie, as might be expected, hauls in the first fish, a small butterfish.

"Not bad!" he says. "Small, but not bad! Good start!"

With that, he rebaits the line and casts again. For some reason or other, Lady Fortune seems to be swimming at the sides of the boat, since every few minutes either Louie or Michael haul in a butterfish or a black sea bream—small but big enough to take home. Both are so busy fishing that they hardly notice that the pair in the rear have long since given up, in fact, they never really started, both of them sitting slightly bent over the back of the boat as if searching to see what kind of creatures might be lurking in the ocean depths. Sensing that a break might be order and seeing, as Paul had said, that they really hadn't had much of a breakfast, Louie opens up a large styrofoam box, takes out a sandwich, and begins to unwrap it.

"Time for a break!" he says, holding up a sandwich. "Salami? Or would you prefer bacon and lettuce? No? How about ham and cheese?"

As he makes the offer, a strangely colored conglomerate mass of mustard, mayonnaise, and ketchup oozes drop by drop from the sandwich. Paul doesn't even look up but, instead, waves his hand as if to say, Dump it! Louie, ever sensitive, doesn't bother asking Akio. Then, remembering something else in the box, he pulls out another sandwich.

"Hey, Paul, how 'bout this: hamburger patty with tomatoes and pickles?"

This time Paul doesn't even wave his hand. Instead, he leans over the side of the boat and makes the strangest kind of sound. Even the cat, heretofore asleep, perks up her ears, wondering why in the world her master is making such strange gurgling sounds. Akio, never one to be left behind, follows in close unison, as is he were mimicking Paul in some kind of ancient Noh drama.

Just around this time, Louie gives a yell. "Hey! Hey! Michael, get the net! Quick! Get the net!"

The rod bends, lets up, then bends again as the fish pulls, gives in, then pulls again. And pull it does: five, ten, a good fifteen minutes. But the fish is tiring and Louie knows that, if the line doesn't break, very soon he'll have it in the boat.

When the fish comes close to the top of the water, Michael scoops the net down, lifts it up, and hauls the fish into the boat. It must weigh a good twelve pounds. But neither he nor Michael have the slightest ideas what kind of fish it is—certainly not a mackerel (too thin), and certainly not a butterfish (too long). It doesn't matter. It's in the boat now safe and sound.

The fish tied tightly to a separate line, Louie happens to glance back again towards the rear of the boat. Paul now has his head in his hands; Akio is sitting on the floor, starring at nothing in particular, unless it be the dim line of the seashore in the distance.

"Michael," says Louie mercifully, "I think it's time."

Michael nods and, with that, begins to gather the gear. Louie then starts the engine and the boat begins to slice through the waves as they head for the shore, making better progress than when they had started. Twenty minutes later, they approach close to the ramp. The owner, seeing them returning, is there to greet them. When the boat siddles next to the ramp, he takes the forward part and pulls it even closer. At this, everyone disembarks, Paul and Akio a bit wobbly, but with a hint of relief in their eyes at being on solid ground.

At this point, Louie reaches for his prize fish and holds it high before the owner's eyes, eliciting an excited response. "Hey, that's some fish! Never saw a barracuda that size before."

"Barracuda? Is that what it is?"

"You bet! They're down in the Inland Sea, but not here. Must have come up with the current. That's some fish! I've been here thirty years and I never saw anything that big. Wait, I'll get my camera!" He hurries to his truck and pulls a small camera from the glove compartment.

"OK! Stand over there near the boat. OK, good! Hold it up! That's it! One . . . two . . . cheese! OK, got it! Hey, you ought to register that fish. It's a record!"

"Thanks," Louie says, "maybe I will. Might have it mounted, too. That'd look great!"

At that, everyone enters the man's truck for the ride back to the van. When the tackle and the catch of fish are arranged in the back, Paul places the cat on a cushion and then secures the leash to a small hook just under the back seat, leaving just enough room for Millie to stretch a bit. Then Paul takes a seat in the back with Akio, while Michael sits beside Louis. Everything in order, Louie starts the engine, glides the van out of the lot, and heads for home.

As various thoughts flow through each one's mind, the van speeds along: from Ise to Tsu, then to Suzuka, Yokkaichi, and on up to Kuwana and a brief stop for a cup of coffee, then on to the final lap to Nagoya. And now, for the first time, Akio begins to open up, joking about some other fishing trips he's made with Louie. Paul, however, remains strangely quiet, not even joining in the laughter at Akio's stories. Then, when they are only a few kilometers from home, he leans over the seat and says to Louie, "Listen, can you let me out at Gokisoo? I want to stop in Lawson's for a second."

"Do you want to buy something?"

"Yes, I'd like to get some cigarettes."

"Cigarettes! For whom? You don't smoke."

"No, but I, ah, I just started a few days ago. Bad habit, but it's too late to stop."

"OK, if you like. Where's the store? I'll take you there."

"Oh, no, it's not necessary. You can stop . . . stop here. It's OK. I can find it OK."

"Stop here? We're not even in Gokisoo yet!"

"I know, I know. I need the exercise . . . sitting so long. . . walk it off a bit." (Pause) "It's OK. Let me off here. It's OK."

With a puzzled look on his face, Louie pulls the van over to the curb. "OK, Paul, as you like."

"Thanks, thanks a lot! See you!"

Paul exits the van, walks to the rear, opens the door and takes Millie, leash and all, in his arms. Not bothering to wave, he quickly walks in the opposite direction. The van then moves on until it reaches Irinaka, where Akio alights. He thanks Louie, says something about meeting him at school on Monday, then heads for his home.

When the van finally pulls up to their residence a few blocks from the subway station, Michael is the first to open the rear door. "Oh, my God!" he exclaims. Whaaaa . . .!" Puzzled, Louie hurries to the back. Both of them stare in disbelief. The plastic bag that held the fish lay torn open, with the smaller fish lying scattered here and there on the floor. Fate seems to have dealt a harder blow to the barracuda, whose head, tail, and backbone were intact, but whose midsection showed a large empty space, most of the stomach having been eaten by a very hungry animal.

For days afterwards, Louie, grieving over the loss of his prize fish, would not be comforted. He had worked so hard and struggled so long to land the fish! What a pity it was, and how sad! But time heals all and so, as the days pass by, he begins to show his usual feistiness. In fact, should one happen to pass through the teachers' common room, one could not help but see a tall figure with a long neck and muscular arms going around and asking anyone who might be present: "Hey, I know a good place for fishing! Wanna go? I'll prepare everything. Dress warmly. It can get pretty chilly out there."

Printed in the United States
By Bookmasters